LASSO MY HEART

Blazing Eagle Ranch 6

PEYTON BANKS

RNR PUBLISHING

"The mark of fear is not easily removed."

— ERNEST GAINES

BLURB

Not all cowboys break hearts—some are here to mend them.

Natoya Grant had sworn off cowboys for good. After two heartbreaks too many, the last thing the fiery schoolteacher needed was another smooth-talking rancher riding in and out of her life. Cowboys were trouble—she knew that better than anyone—and her heart couldn't take another betrayal.

Darnell Murphy, a rugged and irresistible rancher, was as steady as the horses he trained and warm as the sunsets over the Blazing Eagle Ranch. He wasn't afraid of a challenge—and Natoya was worth the work.

Determined to prove that not all cowboys

were cut from the same cloth, Darnell was determined to earn her trust and break down the walls surrounding her heart. Natoya realized she must decide: will she hold onto her fears or take a chance on a man willing to fight for her heart?

"How are you running late?"

Natoya Grant rolled her eyes at the condescending tone of her friend on the phone. Emerson didn't understand that Natoya was never late. She was always leaving at the perfect time—for her. She glanced around her bedroom and couldn't find the shoes she wanted to wear.

"I'm not. I changed my mind on what time I wanted to leave," Natoya muttered. She snatched her phone from the nightstand and moved over to her closet. She slid the door open and bent down to find the pair of flats she was searching for.

It was the second week of school, and everything was going well. Natoya, a sixth-grade teacher, looked forward to this year. Her students were all wonderful, bright young kids. She loved her job, and teaching the young minds of tomorrow fulfilled something in her that she had always yearned for in life. From the time she was a little girl, Natoya knew she wanted to be a teacher.

"Doesn't matter how you put a spin on it, you're going to be late." Emerson snickered.

"Oh, hush up." Natoya grinned. Her gaze landed on the shoes of choice. She frowned, distinctly remembering she had pulled them out of the closet last night. She grabbed them and tossed them down so she could slide her feet into them. "I'll be just fine."

"Well, I was calling because we haven't spoken in a few days. I thought I would catch you before you went to work," Emerson said.

Natoya felt a slight twinge of guilt. She and Emerson had been best friends since ninth grade. Emerson had been the new kid in school, and Natoya had befriended her immediately. They'd been glued at the hip every day since. Not only had they graduated from high school together, they'd even gone to the same college.

Now, because of Natoya, they lived in different towns.

"I'm sorry. I've been super busy. There were some last-minute changes to the curriculum, and I had to do an entire overhaul of my lesson plans, we moved into the renovated part of the building, and with me finally settling into my house—"

"I know. I know. It's just that I miss you. I wish you weren't so far away. Maybe I could come down and we can drink and paint the new house," Emerson said.

The last few weeks had been a blur. Natoya had moved to Shady Springs a year ago. It was a major life decision. It was needed because she had left a certain situation behind and needed a fresh start. Here in Shady Springs, she'd got everything she'd ever wanted. She'd secured an amazing job at the local school district, a fun small town that had a lot to offer her, and now she had recently purchased her own home.

Who would have thought she would have done all of that in the past year?

Natoya sighed and glanced around her bedroom. She hadn't done much to it yet. She was tackling one room at a time when it came to decorating. There were still some boxes that needed to be unpacked, but she was going to take her time. This house was officially hers, and she was going to make it a home. Emme was on to something. They could go shopping for decor for the room, paint colors and stuff.

"That would be fun!" There would be nothing better than spending time with her bestie, drinking and painting. Even though she doubted they would get anything done once the wine got flowing. She could get the spare room together for Emme. "When would you want to come down?"

"Let me look at my work schedule and see when I can put in for. Maybe I could come for a long weekend."

"Well, let me know. I can always put in for a day or two off. I'm sure they could find a sub for me." Natoya walked back over to her bed and snagged her cardigan sweater. She glanced around the room to make sure she had everything. Her gaze landed on something in the corner.

Her shoes.

She glanced down at her feet and gasped.

"What the hell...?" Her gaze moved back to the corner, and she realized she must have purchased the same pair of shoes twice. She fell into a fit of giggles.

"What is it?"

"Oh God. Nothing. Just nothing." Natoya shook her head. She didn't want to mention this to her friend. She would make some slick comment about Natoya's small shopping addiction. She didn't have a true problem, she just had a hard time walking away from a deal. She made her way out of her room. She headed down to the living room where she had left her purse and work bag.

"All right, girl, I'm going to let you go. I just wanted to holler at you this morning." Emme chuckled.

"I promise to call more often. Things should be settling down soon." Natoya grabbed her bags and hightailed it to the kitchen. Her attention landed on the microwave's clock, and she saw she didn't have time to make a cup of coffee. She would just buy some on her way to work. The Shady Beans Cafe was on her way to work, and she could get a bite to eat along with her coffee. She had discovered it not too long after she had moved to Shady Springs and had fallen into love with it.

They ended their call with the promise to speak again soon. Natoya exited through the side door in her kitchen which took her to her attached garage. She slid into her car and soon was driving through her cozy little neighborhood. She turned the music up and needed some motivation for the hours ahead. It was going to be a long day, but she was ready for it.

Natoya felt a sense of calmness while driving through town. The move a year ago was for her own good and peace of mind. She tried not to think of why she'd relocated. She hadn't wanted to leave family and friends, but this new start was what she'd needed. Her hands tightened on the steering wheel as thoughts of *him* came to mind.

She rolled her eyes and pushed him out of her head.

Clifford Neil was no longer going to be an issue for her. Natoya had thought she was madly in love with her ex-boyfriend. When they'd first met, Clifford had been everything she'd thought she would want in a man. He'd been charming, handsome, and said all of the right things she had wanted to hear.

Natoya had a bad streak to her when it came to choosing men, and when she'd started dating Cliff, she'd thought she'd finally found the one.

Boy, had she'd been so wrong about him. He'd been controlling, constantly cheated on her, lacked respect for her, and took her for granted. When she'd tried to leave him, he'd just show up and proclaim that she should forgive him because who else would want her?

Natoya tightened her grip on the steering wheel again and tried to push him out of her mind—again! She blinked back the tears. It had been hard to leave him. He just wouldn't leave her alone. A restraining order was just a piece of paper, and in their town, his family was good friends with the judge so it hadn't meant a damn thing.

Hence why she had moved to Shady Springs for a new start.

She hadn't had a choice. When she'd seen the job listing for a sixth-grade teacher in Shady Springs, she'd taken it as a sign. It was far enough away from home, but close enough she could still go see her folks. The past year had been wonderful. Cliff must have finally got the hint, or maybe he was just caught up in his most recent conquest that he'd lost interest in her.

She felt safe here in Shady Springs. She had found a community that was welcoming, and the town was amazing. Dating was the last thing on her mind. At least not with a cowboy. Every single one she'd been involved with was no good. She should have learned even before Cliff, but she just kept giving each guy a chance, and they all broke her heart.

Eventually, she figured she would dive back

into the dating scene. She did want someone to spend her life with who could not only be her lover but her friend. A partner in life. Someone she would even be honored to have children with.

With Cliff, none of that would have happened. He'd mentioned kids once, and she'd immediately felt sick to her stomach. There was no way she could procreate with that man.

"Stop thinking of him," she murmured.

She pulled into the parking lot of the Shady Beans Cafe and found a spot. It wouldn't take her long to run in and buy what she needed to get her day going. The owner, Nasia, was a nice woman who certainly knew what she was doing when it came to pastries and breakfast. Natoya had yet to order something she didn't like. She killed the engine and snagged her purse. Today was going to be a great day, and she wasn't going to allow anything to ruin it.

"MISS GRANT, DON'T FORGET ABOUT TODAY!" Principal Sims called out as Natoya rushed down the hallway.

Of course the Shady Bean Cafe had been

packed. Everyone in town must be running behind today. The line had practically been out the door.

"Today?" She paused and turned with wide eyes to acknowledge Mr. Sims. She drew a blank on what was today. Had she signed up for a committee or something?

Mr. Sims chuckled and ambled out of the main office toward her. He had immediately taken a liking to her when she'd interviewed for the position. She had come with lots of experience and recommendations from her prior school district. He didn't want her to pass up their small town so he had practically rolled out the red carpet for her. She'd gotten everything she'd asked for when she'd applied, plus a little more in relocation fees to help make sure she was able to find a decent place in town.

"Today starts the week where the Blazing Eagle Ranch will be here for the students. Wade Brooks will be stopping by to help," he said.

"Oh my goodness. Yes. I'm sorry. I just drew a blank. I haven't had my coffee yet." She laughed. She hefted her bags up on her shoulders. Now she remembered. The school hosted various events to expose the children to different career fields. She had volunteered to pitch in. Not that she had to do much but help coordinate getting all of the kids to where they could go outside for the affair.

"That's okay. It looked like you were in a rush." He chuckled again. "Susan will be sending out an email soon to update everyone."

"Thanks for the heads-up. I have a ton of things on my mind and almost forgot," she admitted sheepishly.

"Not a problem. It will be fun. The kids love when the Brooks family brings out their animals. You will enjoy it, too. I need to go speak with Mrs. Thomas for a moment. I'll catch up with you later." He gave her a nod and flagged down another teacher coming down the hall.

Natoya backed away and spun on her heel to hurry to her room.

How could she forget that today would be an all-day field day for the kids? They had been so excited at the end of last week. It was all they could talk about. Apparently, the family who owned the Blazing Eagle Ranch was well known in these parts. The kids spoke excitedly about something called the Kiddie Camp. One of her students, Tyler Brooks, was the grandson of the owner. He was a smart kid who was such a sweetie pie. He was tall for his age and always wore his faithful hat. She'd had to remind him repeatedly that young men didn't wear their hats indoors.

Natoya made it to her room and went inside. She set her things down on her desk and took a sip of her coffee. The long wait for it had been worth it. She was going to need every ounce of caffeine she could get to make it through what was going to be a busy day. The apple Danish she had purchased hadn't made it five minutes in the car before she'd devoured it. Now she wished she had ordered two of them.

She got to work preparing for her students. Field days were always long, exhausting but fun-filled. The kids were going to love the fact that they would be out of the classroom for most of the day. Before she knew it, her students began to arrive.

"Good morning, Miss Grant," a pretty young brunette said who entered the classroom.

"Morning, Tiffany." Natoya picked up her coffee mug and went to stand at her door. She loved greeting her students in the morning as they came into the building.

The foot traffic in the hallway grew as students made their way to their lockers. Middle school was a delicate age group of children. That was why she loved this age group. She always felt they needed more attention during this time. She waved and smiled at students when they passed.

"Morning, Miss Grant." Mr. Roddy from across the hall gave her a nod. He was a thin guy with dark hair and a long, thick beard. The kids got a kick out of his beard that reached midway to his chest.

"Hey, Mr. Roddy." She gave him a wave.

He'd been one of the nice teachers who'd helped get her acclimated to the new system when she'd been hired. He and his wife, Sharon, had been welcoming and had even had her over for dinner.

"Ready for all of the fun and chaos?" she asked.

"Sure am." He gave an eye roll that sent her into a fit of laughter. He shook his head. "At least it's going to be nice out today. I hear it's supposed to be warm."

"Miss Grant?"

Natoya turned her attention to the figure standing by her. Tyler Brooks with his infamous hat on his head stood next to her.

"Now, Mr. Brooks, what have I told you about hats inside?" She leaned her shoulder against the wall and gave him her 'Miss Grant means business' look.

He sheepishly grinned and slid it off. His dark curly hair was thick and pressed down on his head. "I'm sorry. I forgot."

"That's all right. What's up?" she asked. She glanced over at the clock on the wall and saw the kids had about three minutes before the tardy bell rang. Her classroom was already buzzing with excitement. Loud conversations rang out in the hall.

"My uncle is bringing some of the animals soon, and I was wondering if I could go out to help set up?" he asked.

Natoya took a sip of her coffee and eyed the kid. He offered her a pleading look.

She sighed and shrugged. "That should be fine. Put your things away, and when they get here, I'll write you a hall pass to go help," she said.

"Thanks, Miss Grant." He rushed inside the room without looking back.

"I hope you are ready for the smelly farm animals," Mr. Roddy teased.

She wrinkled up her nose at the thought. She had much respect to farmers and ranchers. Cliff had taken her out on the ranch where he'd worked plenty of times. She had always enjoyed getting to be around the animals. Horses always amazed her with how intelligent they were.

She closed off those thoughts. As much as she wanted to remember the good part of their relationship, it was all spoiled by the bad.

"I do love horses. Hopefully they will have a few." She grinned.

The bell rang, and the few students left in the hallway scurried into their classrooms. She snagged the door of hers and tugged it shut behind her. She glanced around and took in all of the bright faces waiting on her. She felt at home here in Shady Springs. This was where she was going to settle down and plant some roots.

"Good morning, class."

2

"Joy, we don't need that many damn sheep," Wade Brooks grumbled. The middle Brooks brother folded his arms in front of his chest while his narrowed gaze honed in on his wife.

"I don't want to hear it, and yes we do. There is nothing wrong with taking three with us," Joy Brooks retorted. She ushered the last of the sheep into the trailer and slammed the door shut behind them. She turned and mimicked her husband. "The kids love when they get to play with the sheep."

Darnell Murphy chuckled as he stared at the married couple. He wasn't going to get in the middle of their bickering. He tipped the brim of his hat back slightly so he could see the sky. They were running a little late. Today was the first day of the Ranching Field Day at the Shady Springs Middle School. Wade had roped him into helping out this year.

"I didn't say they didn't. I just said we don't need three. Why isn't two enough?"

Darnell rolled his eyes. He had known Joy and Wade for a while and didn't understand how Wade didn't recognize the stubborn tilt to his own wife's chin. This was not a battle his friend was going to win.

"We're going to be late," Darnell drawled. He might as well try to help his friend by ending a sure-to-be argument between the two.

Joy glanced over at him with a small smile on her lips.

"Let's go. We are ready." She spun on her heel and headed toward the driver's door of the pickup truck.

"Just where the hell are you going?" Wade stalked after her.

Darnell shook his head and headed over to the passenger side.

"I'm driving," Joy said.

"No, you're not," Wade growled.

Darnell chuckled again and rested his hand on the truck's back door. These two always bickered back and forth, but there was love between them. Their little fights were always the comic relief of the ranch. Joy knew how to test Wade, and Darnell found it hilarious.

He got in and closed the door. The sound jolted the two of them. Joy stepped forward and wrapped her arms around Wade's waist.

"Fine. You can drive."

Darnell turned away from the public display of affection between the two. It was like the arguments fueled something else in their relationship. Darnell took his wide-brimmed hat off and set it down on the seat next to him. He combed his fingers through his hair. He longed for someone to be able to test him the way Joy did Wade. The two of them were perfect together.

The image of Melanie came to mind. He bit back a curse at the thought of his ex-fiancée. He had been in love with her. They had been together for three years before he'd popped the big question. It had been the right time. Everything was going good between them—at least he had thought it was.

Melanie was beautiful. Long auburn hair, big

blue eyes that had drawn him in immediately when they'd first met. He'd been out with a few friends to celebrate one of his longtime friend's, Mark's, birthday. They were out drinking and having fun when Darnell's gaze landed on a beautiful woman sitting at the bar with her friend. He couldn't resist going up to her. They had hit it off immediately. Their relationship had grown fast.

Darnell had wanted everything to be perfect for the day he would propose. He'd worked hard, saved his money to make sure he could offer a woman something. He'd seen how hard his parents worked together and he wanted to ensure that not only would he be offering himself, but security and love as well.

He'd been loyal to Melanie. Not once did his eyes ever stray to another woman. She was going to be his future. She'd even said yes when he'd proposed in front of their family and friends. He'd picked the best time. One of his younger cousins had graduated from college and was home where they were celebrating. The family had thrown a big barbecue in his honor. With Shady Springs being a small town, it wasn't unusual for townsfolk to come out and support, so Melanie didn't suspect anything when her folks were present.

Darnell had gotten down on one knee and proposed.

He'd been nervous as all get out, but it had paid off. She'd said yes.

Only, a year later he'd found out that she'd been seeing someone else.

Darnell inhaled sharply. The pain was still there. His pride had taken a hit. He didn't want to think of the things that had been said between them when he'd confronted her about the rumors that had started circulating around town.

Even with everything he'd gone through, Darnell still held out hope to find someone to spend the rest of his life with. Everyone wasn't like Melanie. He knew that. His heart may have been broken, but it had healed. It had been four years since the breakup. He'd dated here and there since but just hadn't found anyone who he could sense he'd want to spend the rest of his life with.

Still, he held out hope.

Darnell refused to join those online dating apps. He knew some of the other hands had, but most of them were used for hookups. Not that he was judging them or anything, it just wasn't for him. There were a few women he'd dated who he could call on when the itch struck. No strings attached was nice and all, but Darnell wanted to be able to have someone to come home to every night. He was getting older and was beyond ready to settle down. He was forty years old and wanted to still be young enough when it came time to have children.

He wanted to find a woman the old-fashioned way. Get to know her in person. Fall in love. Settle down, have some kids and live life in Shady Springs. It was a great town to raise a family. He loved this town and enjoyed working at the Blazing Eagle Ranch. The Brooks family was a well-respected family in the ranching business and were fair to their employees. He couldn't ask for a better ranch to work on.

Ranching had been his entire life. It was all he knew. Darnell had grown up in Shady Springs. His parents owned a little piece of land on the outskirts of town. His father was a pharmacist at the local drug store while his mother worked at the post office in town as a clerk. His parents had been married since they were nineteen years old. They'd settled down in Shady Springs and had him and his younger brother, Dane. He'd had a great childhood and would love to have what his parents had.

"All right. We're ready to go," Wade announced as he slid into the driver's seat.

Joy was sitting next to him in the passenger seat. Darnell was glad that they had worked out the issue of who was driving. He held back a snort. It really didn't matter who drove them to town. Tyler, the son of the eldest Brooks brother, had been talking about this day for a while and was excited for it.

"It's about time," Darnell joked.

Wade barked a laugh and threw the truck into drive. It wouldn't take them long to get to town. Volunteering to help out gave him a break from working on the ranch. The three of them would be able to handle the animals that they were taking up to the school. Darnell also didn't mind helping educate the young kids about the animals. Many of them may not have been around horses, cows, or sheep, and it was a great way to get the interest of them now. They needed future men and women to join the ranching profession.

Darnell could remember getting exposed to ranch life at an early age. He'd been fascinated with the idea of cowboys as long as he could remember. If someone would have asked seven-year-old Darnell Murphy what he wanted to be when he grew up, he would have responded—a cowboy.

Now look at him.

He'd started working on a small stead when he was fifteen years old. He was a fast learner, and before he knew it, he was working with the horses on Mr. Redmond's ranch. His first job solidified his decision to follow his dreams. He had a connection with horses. There was something about the magnificent animals that drew him to them. They were highly intelligent, dependable, and easy to train. On the Blazing Eagle, he worked with a lot of the new horses to help break them in and even trained some of the ones that were utilized for the kids during Kiddie Camp in the summer.

The ride into town was smooth. The weather was going to be perfect, too. It was a beautiful fall day that called for warm temperatures and lots of sun. The scenery flew by with the fresh air flowing into the open windows. Wade and Joy were deep in conversation about their son, Logan. Darnell ignored them while he rested his head back. It was going to be a long day. He'd arrived at the ranch a little after four to help out before they'd packed up to go to the school.

"We are here," Wade announced.

Darnell blinked and hadn't realized that he had been so lost in his thoughts that he had missed the fact they had traveled through town. Wade slowed down and made the turn into the school's driveway. He headed around to the back where they would set up the exhibits for the animals. There was a large plot of land with an ample amount of trees for the animals to be positioned for the kids to come out and meet them.

The truck drew to a halt. Darnell reached for his hat and plopped it back on top of his head. His gaze wandered over to the large modern-looking school. It had been renovated since he'd walked the halls there as a kid. He had great memories of school. He and his brother were athletes and had a love of sports that they still shared to this day.

"Tyler said he was going to come out and help set up," Darnell said.

He had befriended the young boy. Tyler was a good kid and loved the ranch. He reminded Darnell of himself at that age. From the moment Tyler had stepped foot on the ranch, he'd blended right in as if he had been there his entire life. Everyone knew the story of Parker and Maddie. Darnell couldn't even begin to imagine what Parker had gone through when he had found out he'd fathered a child with the love of his life and never knew it until a couple of years ago.

"Yeah, he bugged the hell out of me this morning before he left for school." Wade chuckled.

They exited the truck and headed toward the back. They paused and took in the field where they would set up. Darnell already had in his mind where he'd be with the horses. They had brought a couple of gentle ones that were great with children.

"I'll go notify them that we are here," Joy said. She spun on her heel and headed toward the building.

Wade's gaze was on his wife. It was easy to see how much he loved her. He turned back to Darnell, his gray-eyed gaze landing on him.

"Let's get started." Wade clapped him on the back.

Darnell followed him toward the trailer and looked forward to getting to educate the students on his favorite animals.

"HEY, DARNELL!" A FAMILIAR VOICE called out.

He turned to find Tyler rushing toward him with a beautiful woman in tow. Darnell's eyes locked on her and froze. The breath caught in his throat at the sight of her. Her tawny beige skin was smooth, her short chin-length hair was dark and tousled as if she'd run her fingers through it. Her large brown eyes and plump lips captivated him. She was slightly shorter than Tyler, and her curves had his mouth watering.

No wonder Tyler loved school. Darnell didn't remember any of his teachers looking like her. If he had, he would never have left the building.

"Tyler, what's up, buddy." Darnell cleared his throat. He tore his eyes off the woman who walked along with Tyler and tried to look at him, but his eyes were drawn back to the beauty.

They'd finished the setup and were ready for the students to come out to meet all of the animals. Darnell had decided to bring his personal horse, Benji, who was highly intelligent, loved attention, and had a soft spot for children. He'd also brought Sasha, a mare who was used in Kiddie Camp. She loved children, and Darnell had trained her himself.

"Miss Grant said I could come out and help. I

wanted her to meet you, Uncle Wade, and Aunt Joy," Tyler said. He stopped a few feet away from Darnell. He smiled wide and rushed over to Benji. "Hey, Benji. I didn't know you were going to bring your horse. You should have brought mine."

Darnell had thought about it for a brief second, but they had been running behind. He was sure Parker wouldn't have cared.

"My bad, buddy. Maybe next time," he said. He smiled and relaxed. He moved over to Miss Grant and held out a hand. Tyler always spoke highly of his teacher. Now Darnell knew why. "Miss Grant, it's nice to meet you. I'm Darnell."

She smiled and took his hand in a firm grip. Darnell's heart skipped a beat the moment her smaller hand slid into his. Her hand was the direct opposite of his. It was tiny and soft. Unlike his that was rough with calluses from hard work.

"Likewise, and please, call me Natoya," she said.

She stepped back from him and reached up and tucked some of her dark hair behind her ear. Her hair wasn't as dark as he'd initially thought. Now she was standing next to him, he could see it was a lighter brown color. It went well with her light-brown complexion.

She motioned to Benji. "Who do we have here?"

"Ah, this is Benji. My personal horse. He loves kids and wouldn't let me leave him behind," Darnell joked.

Her smile widened, and it did a little something to Darnell. He wanted to see her smile and laugh. He motioned for her to join him as he moved over to Benji and Tyler. He grabbed Benji's reins and patted his loyal gelding on the nose. Benji pushed his head against Darnell's. The horse's attention was locked on Natoya who shyly stood in front of him.

"Benji, this is Natoya, Tyler's teacher. Natoya, this is Benji."

She laughed at the introductions but stepped forward and offered her hand out for Benji who bent down and sniffed her hand. Darnell was impressed with how comfortable she appeared to be around horses. She obviously knew she should allow animals to scent her first before just touching them. He patted Benji on his neck. The horse inhaled sharply and snorted. He moved forward toward Natoya in a welcoming manner.

Darnell wasn't surprised. His horse not only had a soft spot for children, but women, too. He was known to be a ladies' man when it came to females—horses or human.

"You are so handsome," Natoya murmured as she ran a hand along Benji's nose.

"He loves attention," Darnell replied. He hated to admit, but he was a little jealous of Benji. Hell, with a beautiful woman like Natoya, he'd take his hat off and allow her to run her hands along his face and hair. He took a quick breath and tried to keep the fantasy of her hands threading themselves in his thick hair out of his mind.

He shouldn't be having such thoughts of his young friend's teacher.

"I'm sure he does." She giggled.

Her big eyes turned back to him, and he felt his breath get snatched from his lungs. They were a deep, dark brown, and it was easy to get lost in them.

"That over there with Tyler is Sasha. She's one of the mares we use for the summer camp. She's another one that was perfect to bring." He motioned over to where Tyler now stood with Sasha. He hadn't even realized Tyler had moved.

"These horses are absolutely beautiful. So I take it you work on Tyler's family ranch?" Natoya asked.

She was still slowly running her hand along Benji's neck who wasn't moving. It looked like Benji had made a new best friend. Darnell stepped back from him and folded his arms in front of his chest.

"I do. I've been with them for a while now," he said. His gaze shifted to her hands, and he didn't see any rings on her fingers. In this day and age, that didn't mean anything. He suddenly remembered Tyler introducing her as *Miss* Grant.

A soft breeze blew, ruffing her hair. She laughed as Benji chose that moment to bump her gently with his head. His horse was definitely winning Natoya over.

"Well, it was nice to meet both of you, but I need to get back to work. I'm sure the kids are ready to come out and have some fun," she said.

She gave Benji another firm pat before she stepped back from him. She smiled at him, and Darnell immediately knew he wanted to get to know her. He didn't recognize her. She must be new to town. Not that he knew every single person who lived in Shady Springs, but Miss Natoya Grant would be someone he would remember meeting.

"It was nice to meet you, Darnell."

"You, too." He swallowed hard and watched

her turn and head back to the school. The gentle sway of her hips mesmerized him. Her jeans looked as if she had been poured into them. He tore his eyes away and stepped over to Benji. He gave his friend a pat. "Listen here, buddy. You can't have all the women."

Benji snorted, and Darnell barked a laugh. He turned his gaze back to the school and found Natoya entering the building.

"She's mine, good friend. Just you wait."

3

"Be nice. The animals aren't going anywhere," Natoya called.

The sun was out, and it was a beautiful day. Natoya pushed her sunglasses higher on the bridge of her nose. She found herself enjoying the change of scenery. It did feel good not to be cooped up in the building for hours. Fresh air and sun was definitely needed.

The kids were loving the field day and getting to meet the animals. The school had arranged for not only the Blazing Eagle Ranch to be represented, but for the local veterinary group who oversaw the medical care of the animals along with a few local farmers to teach about crops and where their food came from. It was a great agricultural lesson for the students, and they were eating it all up. Natoya had even gone around and met a couple of the families from the farms. She loved to cook and had received some invites to come out to the farms to purchase fresh fruits and veggies directly from them.

"Push him again, Richard Hohn, and you will go to the principal's office," Natoya threatened.

Richard was from Mrs. Barker's class, and she'd heard he could be a handful. He glanced over at her and rolled his eyes. Natoya narrowed hers on him. She didn't tolerate disrespect in her classroom.

"Try me."

"Okay," he sighed.

The kid next to him looked relieved that Natoya had intervened. She didn't tolerate bullies and would not hesitate to step in if needed. Richard and the group of youngsters were waiting in line to pet the sheep. The young lady working with the sheep was very enthusiastic when she was talking with the children about the animals.

One of the sheep became very vocal as if to get attention.

"No need to holler, Wilbur. You will get to meet the kids," Joy said. She rolled her eyes and slapped the sheep on the back.

Natoya had met with the woman briefly, and

immediately they had hit it off. Even though Natoya had been in town for a short while, she hadn't met too many people outside of work. Joy seemed to be someone who Natoya could see herself hanging out with. They had exchanged numbers with the promise of grabbing lunch soon.

Joy's talk about her family was interesting. She taught some history of their town. Her family had been one of the first Black families to settle in Shady Springs. They'd raised sheep, and Joy had even talked about barrel racing in her younger days. Some of the girls in Natoya's class lit up at the mention of it. They fell into a big discussion about it. Apparently, a few of them were barrel racers when they were younger.

"Mrs. Brooks. Is it hard to work with sheep?" Natoya raised her hand and asked. She found herself as interested in learning about the animals as the students were. Even though she loved horses, the sheep looked so damn cute.

Her thoughts turned back to Darnell and the horses. Tyler had dragged her out of the classroom so she could meet his uncle, aunt, and friend. He was proud of his family, and she'd agreed, but the moment her gaze had landed on Darnell, all of her wits left her. Thankfully, she was able to focus on the horses. Benji had taken to her immediately and her to him. He appeared to be a gentle soul. His eyes revealed his intelligence. It was obvious that Darnell cared for him.

She sighed. Of course the first man who took her breath away and had her interested was a damn cowboy.

What. The Hell.

She'd asked him if he worked on the ranch to find out. She was hoping he was the vet or someone just helping out.

But nope, he worked on the ranch.

She was done with cowboys and was not going to even entertain the idea of Darnell. No matter how good-looking he appeared in those damn jeans. Or how that damn t-shirt molded to his muscular physique. Or how his brown eyes watched her. He'd had a hat on, but she could see his dark strands peeking out from under it. Was his hair curly? Was it straight? How would it feel to comb her fingers through it?

Lord, what was wrong with her?

Why couldn't he have been a banker or something?

But she knew how it went. He would be nice and charming now, then a fucking asshole with a few screws loose once she really got to know him.

Which was not going to happen. She had made up her mind.

She'd been down that road plenty of times. She was not going to go through that again. Did she know that men who were not cowboys could be assholes and dipshits? Of course she did. But at least she could weed out most if she just avoided one type of man.

She sighed and tried to push Darnell out of her head. Nothing was going to happen between them.

"Actually, it's not. They are easy to get along with and are trainable." Joy laughed.

Natoya's eyebrows shot up in surprise.

Joy motioned to the three sheep and pointed to them as she named them. "That one is Wilbur, the one in the middle is Albert, and that one who can't stop eating every blade of grass is Tiny."

Natoya laughed at the look of Tiny. There was nothing small about that sheep. It was larger than the other two, and Joy was right. He hadn't stopped grazing since they had arrived to hear Joy talk about the animals and her family's farm.

"Having fun?" a deep baritone voice asked.

Natoya's breath caught in her throat. She didn't have to turn to know who was standing next to her.

Darnell.

She glanced over at him and hadn't realized how much taller he was than her. She had to tilt her head back slightly to meet his gaze. There was a small smile playing on his lips. She nodded, and her heart raced.

Down, girl. He's a cowboy, and we know what that means.

"I am," she said. She turned away and eyed the students to ensure they were behaving themselves.

Richard had moved on to a group who were standing over with Mrs. Barker. Natoya relaxed slightly, seeing how he was with his own teacher now.

"This is nice of y'all to come out and educate the kids. I've even learned quite a bit."

She was trying not to look over at him. She didn't want to see the flecks of gold in his eyes. Or the way they crinkled in the corners when he smiled. She tried not to even inhale too deeply. She didn't know what cologne he had on, but it was drawing her to him.

She closed her eyes briefly and sent up a prayer.

"Really? Well, that's good. That's why we do

this. It's also a way for me to get out of work." He chuckled.

He folded his arms across his chest, and in doing that, it allowed her to see how thick his biceps were. Her gaze moved over to his hands, and there was an absence of a wedding ring. She tore her eyes off him and stared straight ahead. A few of the kids were rubbing the sheep and listening to Joy talk about shearing them. Natoya tried to pay attention, but her thoughts kept going back to the man beside her.

"You seemed easy around the horses," Darnell said.

She nodded and smiled. "I have always had a soft spot for them. When I was a kid, I wanted one so bad, but there was no way my family would have been able to afford one." It was silly to think back to the day where she'd cried and begged her father for a horse. How could she not want one? There was this television show she was obsessed with when she was a kid, and after that, she knew she wanted one. "I know it's silly. Most kids ask their parents for a dog, cat, or even a turtle. Me? I wanted a pony of my own."

"Not silly at all. Horses are one of the best pets to own," he replied.

She felt his eyes on her and fought back

glancing over at him. Him being this close to her was ruining her concentration.

"I've had Benji since he was weaned from his mother," he said.

"Really?" This piqued her interest.

She turned to face Darnell. He swept his hat off and raked his fingers through his hair. The dark strands appeared to be thick and silky. Her fingers ached to run through them. He plopped his hat back on.

He nodded over to where the horses were grazing. "If you want to come back and see them, feel free, but I think my break is over." He grinned and tipped his hat to her. He jogged away and headed back over to the horses just as a group of kids were arriving.

Lord, the way that man wore a pair of jeans.

"He likes you."

Natoya jumped. Her face warmed at getting caught ogling Darnell as he walked away.

"He does not," Natoya grumbled.

He was chatting with the group then threw his head back with a laugh. It was easy to see he was comfortable around the students and was enjoying himself. She reached up and tucked her hair behind her ear. She glanced over at Mrs. Barker who had arrived at her side.

"Oh, he does. A man that good-looking has practically the entire female staff breaking their necks to get out here so they can go see the horses." Holly grinned.

"He's just being nice." Natoya sniffed. She snuck another peek over where he was and found him motioning to Benji while he spoke.

"He's barely taken his eyes off you, girl. If I was ten years younger and single, I'd give you a run for your money."

"Oh, please. I'm not interested," Natoya lied. She truly wasn't, but she felt herself weakening against her own rules.

No cowboys.

No ranchers.

No farmers.

Nope. She was not interested in someone like Darnell. She didn't care that the entire female staff at the school wanted to meet him. They could have him. She inhaled and felt she was coming back to herself now he wasn't close to her.

"You expect me to believe that?" Holly snorted. "I know when a man is interested in a woman, and honey, believe me, he's got his sights on you."

Natoya shook her head, not wanting to

indulge Holly any longer. She knew what she wanted in a man, and right now, Darnell wasn't it. He may be good-looking and great with animals and kids, but that didn't mean crap.

"I'm okay. Single life right now is not bad." She shrugged.

The kids who had been speaking with Joy had decided to move on. She stepped forward and brought up a smile. She just needed a distraction. Once field day was over, she doubted she would ever see Darnell again. This may be a small town, but that didn't mean she would run into him again after today.

"Can I pet one of the sheep?"

"Of course." Joy laughed. She waved to the three. "Pick which one you want. They are all lovable."

"Miss Grant!" Tyler called out.

Natoya turned around at the sound of his voice. It was nearing the end of field day. She was exhausted. She'd truly enjoyed herself and got to meet so many people who'd participated to make the day a success. Her feet were sore from standing so much. That was the downside of chaperoning the kids while they were outside. There wasn't much sitting. She promised herself a good soak in a hot bath when she got home.

"Yes, Tyler?" she replied.

He ran up to her, wide grin on his face. She immediately grew suspicious of the look. She could always tell when one of her kids were up to something. This may only be the second week of school, but she had a knack at sensing when her students were acting out.

"Could you come here for a second? Darnell said he had a question for you."

His smile grew wider, and she became even more suspicious. What, exactly, could Darnell have to ask her? She had pretty much avoided him the rest of the day. Whenever he'd made to come toward her, she'd readily busied herself with something with the kids.

Now she was trapped. She couldn't be rude and just say no, could she?

Her mother, unfortunately, had trained her better than that. Maybe he truly did have a question for her. She sighed and gave a slight nod.

"You have fun today?" She walked along with Tyler toward where Darnell stood with his horse.

It appeared to be snack time for the horse.

Darnell was holding on to a carrot while Benji promptly ate it in a few bites.

"I did. You know Darnell is super cool. He's friends with my uncles and my dad. He's one of the best guys who work at the ranch," Tyler announced.

"Really?" she drawled. She suddenly had the sense that her student was trying to play matchmaker between his adult friend and teacher. She eyed Darnell as they arrived near him. She stopped a few feet away from the handsome cowboy and his horse.

Damn it, why did she have to call him handsome?

"Darnell, I told you I could get her over here!" Tyler announced with a wide grin.

Natoya rolled her eyes. She knew it. Darnell didn't have any questions for her at all. Tyler was being a little matchmaker.

She folded her arms in front of her chest and narrowed her eyes on the kid. He probably couldn't see her eyes due to her sunglasses, but she was sure he knew how she was looking. He didn't care. The twelve-year-old fell into a fit of laughter.

"Thanks, Tyler." Darnell chuckled. He

removed his hat from his head and combed his fingers through his hair again.

She bit her lip to keep from sighing out loud. The man was downright sexy, and the move did something to her libido.

"No problem, Darnell. I think Uncle Wade needs help with the cows," he said. He backed away and jogged off toward his uncle.

Natoya whipped her gaze around and eyed Darnell.

"Using a kid, huh?" She pushed her glasses on top of her head.

Darnell burst out laughing and put his hat back on. "Guess I got a little desperate. You've been surrounded by kids for the past few hours." The man had no shame. He'd literally just used a kid to pull a woman over to him. His eyes twinkled as he watched her.

"Well, unlike you, I am at work. This is what I do," she replied haughtily. She already knew what was coming. He was definitely going to be asking for her number or ask her out. She drew up to her full height and felt that she should probably just nip this in the bud now. She didn't want to lead him on. She may have sworn off men like him, but she didn't have to be mean when it came to letting them down.

"I see that. Tyler has talked about you nonstop since the beginning of school. Miss Grant said this and Miss Grant said that." He did a horrible job at mimicking Tyler's voice. His was much deeper than the twelve-year-old.

Natoya couldn't keep the small smile from appearing on her lips. Tyler was a great kid, and he was super smart and helpful in the classroom.

"Well, it's good to know someone is actually listening to me when I'm teaching," she said. She sighed and decided to go ahead and get it over with. "Look, Darnell. I'm sure you are a great guy, but I'm not interested."

The smile slowly faded from his face. Natoya suddenly felt like a bitch. Her words hadn't come out exactly how she'd imagined they would. She just didn't want to play games and lead him on.

"Oh, well...um, damn," he said. He turned and patted Benji on the neck before shifting his gaze back to her. "How do you know without even getting to know me?"

It would be hard to explain to him without insulting him. She didn't want to get a reputation of being a bitch.

"I've just gotten out of a rough relationship and I'm not ready. I don't want to sound mean or anything. I just didn't want to lead you on," she said. She prayed it softened the blow. She backed way, almost ready to sprint to the building so she could hide in her classroom.

"I see," he said.

The way the words fell from his lips sounded as if he didn't believe her. His brown-eyed gaze raked over her, and in that moment she almost regretted shooting him down. She bit her lip and took another step backward, afraid she was going to change her mind.

"Seriously. It's truly not you." A shaky laugh escaped her.

This was definitely going south. She smiled and gave him a wave. She hoped her smile was convincing. She certainly didn't feel like smiling at the moment. Cliff had done a number on her, and she was completely aware that every man who came after him may pay for his sins. She had to protect herself. That was important. It had taken her leaving the town she had grown up in to be able to get peace. Darnell appeared to be nice, but she was not willing to take the chance. It was time for her to go inside. She was sure her students were waiting for her.

"I'm sorry. It was nice to meet you. See you around somctime?"

"Um, yeah. Have a nice day, Miss Grant," he said.

His dark eyes were locked on her. She inhaled sharply at the way he'd said her name. She spun on her heel and began to walk toward the building. The kids were almost all inside. A few other teachers were still rounding them up. She felt Darnell's eyes on her. She fought turning around to confirm if he was watching her. The heat of his gaze was on her, and she knew if she did look over her shoulder he would be staring at her.

Instead, she held her head high and entered the building. This was the best thing for her. She had made rules and promised herself she would never get involved with another cowboy again and she was going to stick to her guns.

4

*S*eriously. *It's truly not you.*

Those words played in Darnell's head. Even a week after the field day at the middle school, Natoya Grant's words haunted him. Someone had done a number on that woman. It was apparent in her eyes. It made him even more curious about her. She had tried to smile while letting him down, but he could easily see that it hadn't reached her eyes.

See you around sometime?

Yes, they would see each other again. He didn't know how, but he'd find a way to see her. Even if he had to go up to the school for an errand or something.

"Darnell."

He blinked at the sound of his name being called. He had been so lost in his thoughts that he hadn't even realized that Rashad was in the barn headed toward him. It was the end of the day, and he was drained. A few of them were supposed to be going down to the Tipsy Cow for a beer, but he was unsure now if he wanted to go.

He reached his hand in his back pocket and pulled out the last carrot he had for Benji. He was surprised his horse hadn't head butted him for his last treat. His horse didn't play when it came to treats.

"What's up, Rashad?" Darnell held the carrot while Benji took two bites then it was gone. He gave Benji another good pet on the head before turning to his friend and coworker.

Rashad, one of the lead hands, grinned at him. He'd worked on the ranch a few years longer than Darnell and was a pretty cool guy. They had hung out multiple times after work, and he did consider Rashad a friend. He was one of the guys on the ranch who knew what had happened between him and Melanie.

At least the real story. There were versions that had circulated around town that had him cringing. Gossip could be really cruel. It was always bad news that spread through a town like wildfire.

"We're heading out to the bar. You still going?" Rashad asked.

Darnell started walking toward him. His body was screaming for him to go home, take a long, hot shower, and grab one of the long-necks from his fridge.

"I don't know—"

"Oh, come on. You have to go. Some of the girls are going with us." Rashad slapped him on the back and barked a laugh.

Darnell smiled at the thought of his friends and their wives hanging out. He didn't mind going with them. The only problem was that he was always the third wheel. If he went, maybe he could see if Zach, one of the new hands, would want to go. He didn't think Zach was married. They had spoken and worked together quite a lot.

"I'm dead tired," Darnell admitted.

They left the barn. The sun was on its way down. It was fall, and the days were growing shorter. He glanced around and breathed in that fresh Colorado air.

"Shit, I am, too. But Yani wants to get out one or two more times while we still have the chance before the baby comes," Rashad said. His grin widened with pride.

Darnell was happy for his friend. Rashad and Yani would make awesome parents.

"When is she due?" Darnell asked.

They slowly strode toward where all of the hands parked their vehicles.

"Next month. Come on. You know you want to hang out with us. Just have a couple of beers then you can go. I will never hear the end of it if you don't come."

Darnell liked Yani. She was perfect for his friend. He sighed and knew that he was going to have a hard time saying no. He could go and have a beer or two. Buy a round for everyone else and then leave. It would be appropriate. He could be there about an hour or two then leave. He glanced down at his watch and gave a nod.

"Sure. Who all is going?" he asked.

"Stan and Nasia, Karl said he and Nykee may stop through, Joy said she and Wade would be there, and I'm not sure about Parker and Maddy."

"Where's Carson?" Darnell asked. He hadn't seen the youngest Brooks brother in a few days.

"Ah, you know when your wife is a superstar, you get to travel the world." Rashad chuckled. "I think I heard that they are in Nashville right now for something."

Carson's wife was country singing sensation Demi Day. Darnell wasn't sure how Carson had pulled her, but he was one lucky guy. The two of them were madly in love. Demi was a down-to-earth girl, too. One would have thought with her celebrity status that she would be stuck up or something, but no. Demi was one of them when she was home and hung out with them.

"All right. You've twisted my arm." Darnell sighed.

"Sweet. We'll all be there in about an hour if you want to go home and jump in the shower or something." Rashad gave him a salute and jogged over to his pickup truck.

If they were all meeting down at the bar in an hour, it wouldn't do him any good to go home. He could shower here. He kept a bag in his truck with extra clothes. There had been plenty of times where he had actually stayed on the ranch in the bunker house. Some days of working the ranch meant early days and late nights.

He didn't mind staying in the bunker house. Some of the other guys did it as well. When it was busy season, it didn't make sense to go home. Plus, if he arrived home, he may not leave.

Darnell went over to his truck and grabbed his duffle bag from the back. He headed over to the bunker house and went into the shower room. A half hour later, he emerged refreshed. The shower had done him some good. The hot water had hit his muscles in just the right spot.

He'd thrown on clean clothes and felt like a new man. He went back out to his truck with a little pep in his step. His stomach gave a growl. He hadn't eaten since lunch. He'd have something at the bar while he was there, too. Maybe going out was best. It was Friday night, and he hadn't had anything else planned.

He jumped in his car and drove toward town. With the windows down and the air flowing throughout his car, he felt much better. He was getting his second wind. He pulled into the parking lot of the Tipsy Cow and had to find a place to park. It was already crowded, and it wasn't late. Everyone must have had the same idea. Get off work and go have a drink or two to start their weekend.

He finally found a space in the back of the lot. He killed the engine and ran a hand along his face. He grimaced at the feeling of the stubble that greeted him. He hadn't taken the time to shave tonight. He'd do it in the morning. This weekend he was off and would relax. He had errands to run, but other than that, he was not going to do anything.

Darnell picked up his keys and cellphone and exited the truck. He walked toward the bar. The door opened, and people spilled out of the establishment. The loud thumping of music immediately greeted him.

"Derek," Darnell called out as he arrived at the door.

The bouncer eyed him and gave him a nod.

"Darnell." Derek grabbed the door and held it open for him. The bouncer was a huge mammoth of a man.

Darnell jogged up to the door and entered.

"I want a quiet night from you and your friends," Derek said.

Darnell rolled his eyes. It had been a long while since anyone from their ranch had created any problems at the Tipsy Cow. Mainly the Brooks brothers. Darnell couldn't help the grin that appeared. The men he worked for didn't play games when it came to respecting their name and the people they cared about. He'd heard of plenty of stories of the Brooks brothers causing trouble at the bar.

Darnell was more laid-back than most. He

ambled through the bar and scanned the tables until he found a few familiar faces. If the girls were out with them, then he was sure his friends would be behaving.

"Darnell! You came!" Yani exclaimed. She stood from her seat at the table. Her stomach was round and large.

Darnell's eyes widened. She'd gotten even bigger since the last time he'd seen her.

"I did. Your husband twisted my arm to make sure I did." He chuckled.

She wrapped him up into a tight hug as much as her stomach would allow.

"Good. You don't need to be at home by yourself. You should be out with friends," she said. She made her way back to her chair and lowered herself onto it.

Darnell had a new appreciation for women and their bodies. Rashad said she had another month to go. He didn't know how the baby was going to grow any more. Yani looked as if she were going to pop any minute.

"That's right," Nasia said. She sat on Stan's lap with a wide grin on her face. By the glaze of her eyes, she was already a couple of drinks in.

Darnell glanced down at his watch. Rashad had said an hour, and he was on time.

Darnell reached over and shook Stan's hand. They had both worked today but hadn't seen each other. They had been spread out in different pastures. The Blazing Eagle Ranch was one of the largest in the state of Colorado. There was always the chance he wouldn't see one of his friends while at work.

"Stan," he greeted him.

Stan grinned and shook his hand firmly. His wife, Nasia, refused to budge to allow him to stand. Darnell chuckled at her antics.

"He didn't want to come, and I made him." Nasia snickered. She wrapped an arm around Stan's neck and dropped a kiss on his forehead.

It was good to see Stan happy. He deserved it. Darnell had thought he'd had it bad with Melanie. At least his ex was sneaky bitch. From what he'd heard, Stan's ex had been the queen of bitches. Nasia was perfect for Stan. The two of them were in love.

"I never said I didn't want to come," Stan drawled. His lips tilted up in the corner as he met his wife's eyes.

"Hell, I didn't, but Rashad has a way of making you feel guilty if you don't," Darnell said.

They all shared a laugh. Wade and Joy along with Karl and his fiancée, Nykee, were at the table as well. He nodded to them before turning and flagging down a server. He asked for an additional chair to be brought over. Their table was large enough to squeeze one more in.

"Who lays on guilt?" Rashad came up behind him.

"You, you son of a bitch. You knew I wanted to go home and crash," Darnell grumbled.

"Ah, what are friends for? You need to come out. You can sleep later," Rashad said. He held up his long-neck in the air.

"Amen to that," Wade said.

Joy nudged him in the side. With their addition to the family, it wasn't that often the two of them usually came out to hang. Darnell grinned at them.

"Here you go. What can I get you started on?" the server said. She popped the chair down for him and reached for her pad.

He placed a quick order. He was famished and needed food. If he was going to hang out with them then he was going to need food.

"So what's been going on with you, Darnell? I feel like I haven't seen you in a while," Yani said.

All eyes turned to him. He gave a shrug. There wasn't really much to tell.

"Not much. Work and fixing a few things out at the house," he admitted.

"Well, don't forget about the Harvest Festival," Yani said.

The women all nodded. His gaze landed on Nykee. She was always quiet when they all hung out. He didn't know much about her, but everyone always talked about how nice she was. He'd heard there were some things in her past, but Darnell was never one to listen to gossip. He knew on a personal level how much it could hurt to have people talking behind your back.

"I hear it's going to be fun. They hired this popular DJ from Colorado Springs," Nykee said. She had on a tank top that highlighted all of the tattoos that lined her arms. She was a pretty girl, and Karl only had eyes for her.

"I heard that, too. I am ready to dance," Nasia said.

"Seriously. What about you, Darnell? Are you ready?" Joy asked.

The girls all turned their eyes to him. He grimaced and knew they would never let him live a certain night down. At Carson's wedding, they'd all learned that he could not dance. He was proud of his two left feet.

The girls had tried to teach him a few things,

but he just was not a dancer. Nod his head to the beat of a song—sure, he could handle that. Move his body to that same beat—hell no.

"I am not dancing."

The girls fell into a fit of laughter. Wade tried to hide his laughter behind his hand and a cough. Stan lifted his beer and took a long drag from it while Karl and Rashad openly laughed along with the women. Darnell wasn't ashamed of his default. There was plenty else he was talented at.

"Okay, okay." Joy lifted a hand and wiped the tears from her cheeks.

Darnell grabbed his beer and sipped.

"What about line dancing," Joy suggested. "That should be easy. I'm sure if we asked, the DJ would throw on one or two."

Darnell grimaced. Line dancing called for memorizing steps and could get really complicated. His mother was one who knew all of the old and new dances. He never knew how she could get up and just go with the flow whenever one came on.

"I don't know." He shook his head.

"Oh, come on. Why don't you try one dance? I'll go and have him put on an easy one," Yani said. She practically danced in her seat with her eyes full of mischief.

"No, I'm good." He held up his hand and glanced over at Rashad.

His friend had the nerve to be looking at the ceiling. Darnell snatched a napkin from the table and crumbled it up. He tossed it over at Rashad who barked a hefty laugh.

"There's a class, you know, for people who want to learn line dancing. It's in a little studio a few doors down from my shop," Nykee said. She was the owner of What the Fluff, a dog grooming business. She smiled and nudged Karl with her shoulder. "I just signed me and Karl up to take a class."

"Say what now?" Karl sputtered.

Darnell snickered at the look of horror on his face.

Nykee leaned over and kissed him on the cheek. "Now, babe, you know I'm okay with an easy ol' two-step. I don't need to learn line dancing."

"Oh, come. It would be fun." Nykee giggled. "That's why I didn't tell you at first. It would give you more time to try to get out of going."

"Darnell, you should sign up for it. There's going to be a huge line dancing contest, and all of us are entering into it. You should do it. I'm sure you'll like it," Nasia said.

"Why don't you come with us? There's a class tomorrow," Nykee said.

"I'm not entering no contest. I can sit back and watch y'all," Darnell said.

"Oh, don't be a chicken. You never know who you could meet at a dance class. I'm sure there are plenty of single women who go to places like that," Yani said.

Darnell glanced around at the guys at the table. None of them were sticking up for him. It seemed like he wasn't going to get any help there. The girls would never leave him alone. If Karl was going to the class, then he could at least go for moral support of his friend.

"Who said I was wanting to meet anyone?" he grumbled.

"You couldn't take your eyes off Tyler's teacher last week. Why don't you go and ask her out?" Joy said.

All eyes turned to him again. He ran a hand along his face and grimaced. He didn't want to keep being reminded of how she had shot him down.

"Who was it?" Yani asked.

"There's that new teacher. I think her name is Latanya? Or Latoya?" Joy frowned.

"It's Natoya," Darnell said.

He immediately regretted answering. The girls shared a look, and he could see he was in trouble.

He sighed. "And don't get any ideas. She already shot me down. She's not interested."

"I've met her a few times. She comes into my bakery, but she's not interested? What's wrong with her?" Nasia asked.

Stan barked a laugh and kissed the back of her hand. It wasn't anything that he hadn't already thought about a million times since that day. He shrugged.

"She said she just got out of a bad relationship," he shared.

They all seemed to accept that answer. Hell, even he knew what that felt like after the breakup with Melanie.

"Okay, well, back to the class. You want to go? I can call and add your name with ours. I believe there is still room," Nykee offered.

"We should go, too," Joy murmured to Wade.

"Absolutely not. Plus, I know how to do a few dances." Wade leaned back in his chair and rested an arm on the back of his wife's.

His comment didn't go unanswered. Her pestering of him to go with her was just getting started.

"Fine. I will go. One class only, and that's it," Darnell muttered. He lifted his glass and tried to ignore the girls cheering him on. He didn't know what he had got himself into, but he was only doing one class. He didn't care that the Harvest Festival was coming up. He had planned to go and hang out, but he wasn't entering any dance contest. It was a big deal in town, and everyone would be there.

His mind went to the sexy schoolteacher who had captivated his attention last week. He wondered if she was going to the festival. He was determined to talk with her again. She may not be ready to be in a new relationship at the moment, but that didn't mean they couldn't get to know each other. They could start out as friends. There was nothing wrong with making new friends.

Darnell was a very patient man. A woman like Natoya would surely be worth the wait. The memory of her smile and her curves had stayed with him. Determination set in. He wasn't sure who had hurt her in the past, but he would show her that not all men were the same.

A popular song came on that grabbed the girls' attention. Their shouts and excitement filled the air. They all got up and raced toward the dance floor where others had already joined in with dancing. Nykee walked behind with a slower Yani, but they made their way to where Joy and Nasia had raced off to. Darnell swung his attention to the men still seated at the table.

"So none of y'all were going to save me from line dancing classes?"

5

Natoya walked through the doors at the Move and Grove Studio where she taught a class. She had a love of dancing, and with her being a teacher, the two went hand in hand. She'd signed up to teach the class a month ago and was having so much fun with it. She had a knack for it and could easily pick up the latest trends. Her family was notorious for line dancing. All of her life she had experienced her family members enjoying the latest line dancing at parties, weddings, cookouts...anytime they could get up on the floor, they did.

When she'd seen the ad for the position, she couldn't resist. She had fallen in love with the class the minute she'd taught her first one. The townsfolk came out in droves, and her class was usually packed.

"Hey, Natoya!" Missy, the studio's receptionist, called out from behind her counter.

"Hey, hun. How are you?" Natoya hefted her bag up on her shoulder and smiled.

It was a beautiful Saturday, and it was the perfect day for the class. Too bad they couldn't be outside. If she could move the stereo system outside, she would. There was a nice little park-like area behind the building.

"I'm good. Clare's class finished a few minutes early. So you should be good to set up," Missy said.

"Perfect." Natoya breezed past her and headed to the room where she'd be teaching.

The studio was large enough for two classes to take place at the same time. There were aerobics' classes, a spinning one, and a few different types of dance classes. It was a very busy facility that certainly drew the interest of the townspeople of Shady Springs.

Natoya entered her room and saw that Clare had indeed finished early and was already gone. The room was spacious with a mirrored wall and hardwood floors. She went over to the table in the corner and set her bag down. It had a modern

Bluetooth stereo system where she could stream music from her cellphone. She quickly got her playlist ready for class and ensured her phone was connecting properly. She did a test of the system and played some upbeat music. She lowered the volume and grinned. Today was going to be fun.

She was dressed casually in leggings and an off-the-shoulder t-shirt. She expected to sweat a little so she had thrown a headband on to keep her hair from falling forward into her face. She encouraged her students to dress in something they would feel comfortable dancing in. It didn't take long before a few ladies entered the room. Natoya recognized them from her last class. They had giggled the entire time and had a blast.

Some people came already knowing the basic line dancing, while others had never done it before but wanted to learn. Being a middle-grade teacher had taught her patience. Some of her dance students were absolutely horrible, knew it, but didn't care. That's what made the class so much fun.

"Afternoon!" she called out. She reached over into her bag and pulled out her giant water bottle. She took a quick swig then pointed over to the small table by the door. "Please make sure you sign in. Thank you!"

The class was supposed to be filled today. She took another sip of her water before setting it down on the table. She moved around the room to greet people when they came in. Young, old, women and men came to her class. Natoya's smile was wide as she introduced herself to everyone. She called out another reminder for the newcomers to sign in and made her way toward the front of the class. She eyed the room, and excitement filled her. She glanced down at her watch and saw they had another five minutes before they were to start.

"Hello, everyone. I'm Natoya Grant, and I'll be your instructor today. There is only one rule that I ask everyone to abide by, and that is to have fun! No matter how bad you are at dancing, no one here will judge you. Is that right?"

The class all clapped and agreed. There was no judgement when it came to learning to dance. Some caught on quicker than others. This was to be a way for people to get out of the house, meet their fellow townspeople, and learn to dance.

"Also, if you didn't bring water, there is a water fountain at the end of the hall, as well as restrooms. If you get tired and need a break, I do ask that you move off to the side and rest until you can jump back in," she said. She paced slightly as she spoke. It was a habit of hers. She was ready to get started and finish so she could go out and enjoy the rest of her day. Afterward, she had planned to do a little shopping then stop and grab some dinner before heading home. "Are there any questions before we get started? We have a couple minutes."

She eyed the group and recognized Joy, Tyler's aunt, and Nasia from the Shady Beans Cafe. They was accompanied by another woman who Natoya didn't recognize. She gave Joy a little wave and a smile. Joy returned it with a wide grin.

No one had any questions, so she encouraged everyone to take a good sip of water while she pulled up the first song. She walked over to the table where her phone was. A motion by the door caught her attention. She snagged her phone and went to encourage the person who had just arrived to sign in, but her words died on her lips.

Darnell.

What the hell was he doing in her class? Her mouth opened and closed. She was frozen in place. Joy and the women she was with grew excited and ushered him over to their group. He was dressed in jeans, a t-shirt, and a worn pair of cowboy boots. Instead of a wide-brimmed hat, he had a baseball cap on. Their eyes connected, and her heart skipped a beat.

"If you are just arriving, please make sure you sign in when you get a chance," she finally was able to spit out. She yanked her water bottle and took a sip to wet her suddenly dry mouth. She opened her phone and switched the music to an old but goody dance that everyone should know. She wanted to get a feel of where people were, and it always helped loosen them up to start off with one they knew. "Everyone know this one?"

"Yeah!" people shouted and began to clap and rock to the beat.

"All right. Let's see what you can do!" Natoya called out.

She moved to the front of the class and turned her back to them. With the mirror in front of her, she could keep an eye on the class. Her smile widened as most of the room followed along with her. There were a few exceptions where someone would turn right when they were supposed to go left.

But there was one person who was completely out of their element.

Darnell.

The women with him were almost crying from laughter. They tried to guide him with the right steps but were having a hard time getting him to go with the flow.

Natoya bit back a giggle. She wondered what the women's relationship to him was. He seemed to know them and was comfortable with them. Natoya felt a twinge of emotion she was unfamiliar with. She knew Joy was married to Tyler's uncle, but she didn't know about the other ladies with her. There was a pretty one with plenty of tattoos on her arms that was holding his arm while she tried to get him to move with her. Natoya walked around the room and helped others. She tried not to stare at Darnell. He already had help, so she tried to push him out of her mind and guide an older gentleman with steps.

"Kick, kick." She smiled at him.

She went along with him to help show him which leg to kick first then the other before they were to turn. He laughed and shook his head but he wasn't giving up. They turned, and he stepped in the right direction.

"Good job!"

The song ended with cheers and claps. Natoya jogged to the front of the class and faced everyone.

"How'd it go?" she asked.

Chuckles and groans filled the room. It was to be expected.

Natoya grinned wide at the replies that floated through the air. "Keep taking my class and you'll be an expert soon."

She grabbed her phone and chose the next song. This one was a popular one that was gaining notoriety on social media. She'd seen plenty of people doing it and thought it would be fun. It had a country twang to it and should fit right on in. She quickly explained the dance.

"Anyone know this one?" she asked. A few hands went up. She waved for them to come forward. "Come on up here. Let's show them first so they can see how to do it."

A couple of women and a guy came forward to line up with her. She had them face the mirror so they were all standing in the same direction. This would enable those watching to try to jump in. It always helped to demonstrate first when learning new steps.

"Wish I had a fan for this one," the woman with the tattoos who was helping Darnell muttered.

Natoya chuckled thinking of all the videos she'd seen where people were showboating doing the dance and had hand fans to go along with the words of the song.

"All right. We'll do some rounds then we'll pause so you can join in." Natoya started the song and got in line with the others.

They began moving together in sync. Natoya couldn't stop smiling while she danced. Darnell had his eyes on her. She didn't have to look over her shoulder or even in the mirror to know this. She felt the heat of his stare on her. The entire room had their eyes on her and the people helping to demonstrate.

But this was different.

She tried not to look his way in the mirror but failed. Their eyes connected, and for one brief moment she felt as if she were dancing for him only. She couldn't help the extra sway that seemed to appear in her hips. Or raising her arms as she spun with the others.

He stood in place, his gaze not diverting from her.

She held up her hands to signal for the demonstrators to pause.

"Ready to try?" she asked.

Some of the class had been dancing with them trying to learn the steps while others were deer caught in headlights. Darnell's expression was hard to read. Joy elbowed him and whispered something to him that caused him to look away from Natoya.

"I want you all to remain up front. I'm going to go around and help."

They all nodded and smiled. It always did help to have people in the class who knew certain dances. People who came to classes such as this naturally helped each other. Natoya started the song over, and they all began moving to the beat. She walked around casually, stopping to help someone here and there. She finally made it to Darnell's side who was still struggling even with the simple part of the dance.

"It's forward twice. Just listen and catch the beat," she said.

Natoya rested her hands on his arm. A warmth radiated from him. She could sense the strength of him from just that small touch. Her breath caught in her throat as they gazed at each other. Her lips turned up slightly in the corners.

"Were you talked into coming?" she asked.

"How'd you guess?" he muttered. He paused and blew out a deep breath. He took his hat off and combed his hair with his fingers. He motioned to the room. "This is not for me."

"Are you having fun?" She stopped and stood next to him.

He glanced over at the women who were with him. A smirk appeared on his lips.

"A little," he admitted.

"Seriously? I saw you laughing while your friends were trying to help you." She didn't know if the tattooed woman was his friend or more. She seriously hoped he wouldn't have been trying to talk to her if he was already with someone. To be honest, she wouldn't be surprised. Cliff certainly didn't know the meaning of being faithful, and she doubted most other men in his profession did.

She blinked and tried to shake that line of thought out of her brain. She knew it wasn't right, but she had to protect herself.

"I know, but dancing isn't my strong suit," he replied. His gaze swept over her swiftly.

She would have missed it had she not been staring at him. She cleared her throat and almost forgot they were in the middle of class.

"Well, if you want extra help, I can stay afterward with you to give more pointers," she offered. The words came tumbling out of her mouth before she could even stop them.

"He does need help, Natoya." Joy laughed. She came over to them and gave him a friendly push.

Darnell rolled his eyes.

"I'm not entering no contest with y'all. Just forget it," he muttered. He pulled his cap down tighter on his head.

Natoya felt herself soften at the thought of him coming here to please his friends. She glanced around at the women he was with. They were having fun dancing to the music.

"Well, the offer still stands." She spun on her heels and headed back to the front of the class just as the song came to an end.

Claps and cheers went up in the air. She had noticed that some of the dancers who had stumbled at first had caught on. She snagged her water bottle and held it up.

"How about we take a quick water break."

The class began dispersing. She went over to her table and snagged her towel from her bag and wiped her brow. Only a little sweat had formed. She needed to busy herself and not be preoccupied with Darnell. He probably wasn't going to stick around for extra help. She normally stayed after for ten to fifteen minutes to help anyone who needed a few extra tips. Unable to resist looking, she caught the back of Darnell just as he left the classroom.

Slight panic filled her. Would he come back? She didn't know why she was worried about him. He'd already said that dancing wasn't his strong suit, but what was?

She paused before taking another sip of her water. Her mind raced with the possibilities. Just because he couldn't follow a line dance didn't mean he couldn't perform any other way.

Her heart sped up with the thought of him performing another way.

She blinked as an image of him and her came to mind, and it certainly wasn't dancing vertically.

Get your mind out the gutter.

She set her bottle down on the table. Talking with some of the students would keep her mind from wandering to inappropriate visions of Darnell. At the end of the break, she called for everyone's attention from the front. Her gaze swept the room and landed on the women who were with Darnell. They were all present. Except for him.

"All right, everyone. Let's get started again." She smiled.

Her eyes went to the door, but there was no sign of Darnell.

"THE WAY YOU TEACH MAKES IT SO EASY TO catch on," Judy said. The older lady had attended several of Natoya's classes. She was a robust woman with salt-and-pepper hair. Her cheeks were rosy from dancing, and her smile was wide.

Their time had come to an end, and a few people had stayed and were chatting around the room. Natoya held on to her towel after wiping her face. They had kicked it up a notch and had gone on to some other dances that really got one's heart pumping.

"Thank you. It's all about having fun really. Whether you memorize every step or not. This is also a great exercise for you, too," Natoya replied.

Her gaze went to the door again. Darnell hadn't come back in after the break. His friends had remained their goofy selves and carried on without him.

"It is. That's why I come. This is definitely better than aerobics." Judy laughed.

Another woman came over to stand with them. She too had attended a class before. Her name slipped from Natoya's mind.

"Oh, it certainly is. I'm so glad they got you to

teach this class," the other woman said. She patted Judy on the shoulder. "You certainly were moving today."

"I felt great today, and me and Phil got some good news. Donna, I'll share with you after class. We can grab a bite to eat. After all that dancing, I'm famished," Judy said.

"That's a good idea. I think I burned enough calories for the entire week." Donna chuckled. She looked around the class before leaning in to Judy.

Natoya glanced down at her watch and saw the time. If she were to stick to her schedule then she needed to go so she could keep up with all the things she had planned for the day. She excused herself and threw her belongings back into her bag, but she couldn't help but overhear Donna and Judy's conversation.

"That poor boy. It's good to see Darnell out and smiling," Donna whispered.

At least what Natoya was sure she thought was a whisper. She froze and snagged her phone and acted like she was looking at something. What was wrong with Darnell?

"I know. After the way that girl did him, I'm surprised he's out and smiling."

Now Natoya's curiosity was piqued. She

opened up her email and scrolled through it like she hadn't already checked it that morning. There were a few advertisements that had come through that she immediately sent to the trash. Her eyes may be down on her phone, but her ears were wide open as she eavesdropped.

"I just don't see how that girl left him like that. Darnell is a good boy. His momma, Amelia, raised him right. Just because he isn't rich doesn't mean he can't be a good husband," Judy muttered.

Husband? Natoya's head jerked around at the two women walking over to where their things were. Other stragglers were still in the room having conversations.

Had Darnell been married and his wife left him?

Sympathy grew in her heart at the thought of someone hurting him. She knew all about the pain of heartbreak. Cliff hadn't been her first boyfriend who had done a number on her. But he was going to be the last.

Natoya grabbed her bag and lifted it onto her shoulder. As much as she wanted to stay around and listen to their conversation, she did need to go. She glanced around the room to see if there was anything she needed to straighten, but there wasn't anything. A cleaning crew came in after hours and took care of the building.

Judy and Donna exited the room. The last tidbit that Natoya caught had her heart stuttering.

"And I heard he found her with the other man. What kind of woman does that?" Donna whispered.

Natoya froze in place. He'd been cheated on? She closed her eyes briefly and felt her heart cracking. Maybe he wasn't the same as Cliff and the others before him.

What was she doing?

She shook her head and knew she was falling into the same pattern. She had a weakness for a man in tight-fitting jeans, boots, and a killer smile.

She needed to get her head examined.

Natoya gave a wave to the couple still speaking and left the room. She would push Darnell out of her mind. There were plenty of fish in the sea. She may have to deep dive to find the one for her, but she would be willing. She quickly exited the building and walked toward her car. A lone figure stood by a pickup truck a few spots over from her vehicle.

Natoya's heart stuttered. She had thought

he'd left. Darnell hadn't come back into the classroom after the first break, but there he stood with his arms folded and his eyes on her. She gave a small nod and headed toward her car.

"Natoya!" his deep voice rang out.

She arrived at the driver's door and paused. She glanced over her shoulder and watched him amble over to her. His baseball cap was low on his forehead. She wanted to remove it and run her fingers through his hair so she could see his entire face.

"Darnell." She cleared the sudden grit from her throat. She tightened her grip on her bag and tried to push down the butterflies that were fluttering around in her stomach. The man didn't have any business looking as good as he did. His chest was broad and stretched out his dark t-shirt. She wondered what he would look like without that damn t-shirt? She bit her lip and dragged her thoughts away from the danger territory. "What's up?"

He paused when he arrived at her side. He glanced away for a moment before focusing on her again.

"I just wanted to apologize," he said.

Her eyebrows shot up. There was nothing for

him to apologize for. She tilted her head to the side and studied him. "For what?"

"For just leaving like I did. I only came because the girls wouldn't accept no for an answer. They apparently think I need to learn to dance," he admitted sheepishly. He raised his hat and raked his fingers through his dark strands.

Natoya's breath caught in her throat at the move. It was so damn sexy and was sending her body into overdrive.

"It's okay. Not everyone can catch on, but the main thing about line dancing is that you have fun. Getting wrong steps is fine. No one is perfect," she said.

"You seem to be. You didn't miss one step." He grinned.

"I have been dancing since I was born." She found herself smiling along with him. She reached up and brushed a wayward strand of hair from her face.

"So you are telling me you were dancing before you could walk?"

"Basically. My mother loved dancing, and I'm sure she was dancing every day of her pregnancy with me." She giggled.

Which was true. Victoria Grant did have a love for dancing. Natoya had fond memories as a child of her mother blaring music and dancing around the house as she'd cleaned. She'd always brought Natoya in, and they'd be dancing together while doing chores.

"I'm surprised my mother hasn't taken your class yet. She knows every damn dance out there," he muttered.

His smile widened, and it was then she noticed the tiny dimple that appeared on his right cheek. She swallowed hard and tried not to notice little details about him.

"Well, you didn't need to apologize for leaving the class." She turned to grab the handle to her door, but his warm hand on her shoulder stopped her.

"I actually wanted to make up for it."

"You don't have to. It's okay. Really it is. Plenty of people leave the class before it ends."

He hadn't removed his hand, and she didn't feel the need to step away. His large hand actually felt right. She inhaled sharply.

"Call it my home training, but I do want to show some appreciation for you trying to teach me even though I failed miserably. How about something simple. Just as friends. We can go horseback riding. I can pack a light lunch for us, and we can just have some fun with the horses."

His hand finally slid away, and she had to admit she missed it and wanted it back on her. She tilted her head back and felt her walls cracking. He wasn't fighting fair. How did he know that horses would be her weakness? He did say as friends. Women and men could be friends.

Right?

Just thinking of being on the back of her favorite animal had her folding.

"Okay. When do you have in mind?" she asked.

"How about tomorrow?" His grin spread from ear to ear.

Her heart did a little pitter-patter at the sight of him. There was nothing sexier than a man who was relaxed and enjoying life. No one needed to be serious and grumpy. There was too much good in the world.

"Tomorrow I can do."

6

Darnell felt the tremors in his hands and barked a laugh. He tightened his grip on the steering wheel and guided his truck along. He hadn't been nervous about picking up a woman since he was about sixteen years old. He knew he was going to have his work cut out for him when it came to asking Natoya to spend the day with him. A blind man could see the walls she had built up around herself.

The memory of the way she was around Benji had him realizing that his horse would be the way to get close to her. He wasn't above using Benji as his wingman. His horse had been by his side through the good times and bad. And with all the carrots and apples he'd provided Benji, he'd say his horse owed him.

Yesterday he'd waited around for the class to end. Joy and the girls had come out and found him in his truck. They were curious as to why he was still there. They had even offered to take time to keep working with him, but he'd declined. He knew when to take a loss. They should have known from the wedding. After they had got in their cars and left, he wasn't sure if Natoya was going to leave the building yet.

But the moment she had stepped out of the studio, his nerves had grown. The woman was downright beautiful and took his breath away. The way she had worked with everyone in the class, he could tell teaching was as natural to her as the act of breathing. She was patient and ensured everyone had a great time. Maybe he should have stayed, but he didn't want to embarrass himself any more than he already had.

After she'd agreed to spend the day with him, they had exchanged numbers. He had to remember that he had made the offer of them just being friends. It had been hard not to call her that night. It would have been a creep move, so instead, this morning he'd sent her a text to confirm, and when she did, he'd let her know what time he would pick her up. She had tried to offer to meet him out at the Blazing

Eagle Ranch, but he'd insisted on picking her up.

Of course, he had an alternative motive for it. He wanted to spend time with her to get to know her, and even though this wasn't a date, he still wanted to be a gentleman and pick her up. Something told him she wasn't used to certain things. When he'd opened her car door for her, the way her eyes widened at the act told him everything he needed to know.

Darnell was a patient man, and he was going to take his time in wooing Natoya Grant. She wouldn't realize what had hit her.

He guided his truck onto her street. It was a cozy part of Shady Springs that was not too far from their downtown. It was a nice residential area with well-manicured lawns and homes. He pulled into her driveway and killed the engine. Her car was parked in front of her garage. He blew out a deep breath and pushed down his nerves.

He'd tussled with ornery bulls and pissed-off horses and hadn't broken a sweat. Now that he was about to have a day with the woman who consumed his every thought, he felt like a teenage boy going on his first date.

Darnell had packed them a simple lunch with

cold-cut sandwiches, chips, cookies, and drinks. He knew exactly where he'd take her once they got to going. The Brooks family's land was one of the largest spreads in the entire state of Colorado, and there were plenty of beautiful areas one could enjoy.

He exited his truck and jogged up the stairs to her porch. He pressed the doorbell and stepped back. Natoya must love flowers because there were a few large potted ones sitting on the porch. He glanced around and took in the beautiful day. It was late morning, and it was already warm out. The sound of the door opening had him turning back around. He paused when Natoya came into view.

Her chin-length hair was doing its feathered thing that made it appear full while she had one side tucked behind her ear. She was dressed in a t-shirt that stopped slightly above her belly button and jeans that looked as if she were poured in them. Her skin practically glowed, and her eyes held a twinkle in them.

"Hey," he said.

He coughed to try to clear the frog that suddenly appeared in his throat. He stepped back as she opened the screen door and came out onto the porch. The scent of her perfume hit him. He inhaled sharply and immediately memorized it as her scent. There was a hint of coco butter and warmth to it. He had to resist the urge to gather her to him and nuzzle his face into the crook of her neck where he could breathe her in. He doubted she would appreciate that.

Friends didn't do things like that.

"Good morning," she murmured. She raised her purse on her shoulder and turned to lock the door.

He held the screen door for her, and once she was done, he closed it.

"So you have a horse for me?" she asked.

He grinned and motioned for them to go to his truck. They arrived at the passenger door where he opened it for her.

"Yeah. I already called ahead, and they will be ready for us when we get there," he said. He helped her up into the truck before shutting the door. He jogged around to his side and hopped in. "Have you ridden before?"

He started the engine and backed out of the driveway. Talking about riding should keep his thoughts from going down the road of them being naked and entwined together.

"It's been a while," she said sheepishly. She reached up and re-tucked her hair behind her ear.

The windows were down and allowed the fresh air to come inside, but all Darnell could smell was Natoya. Her perfume or lotions filled the cab of his truck. He breathed in and had to beat down the urge to adjust his stiffening cock.

"As a kid, I had a friend who had a few horses, and she taught me," she said. "We'd go riding almost every weekend."

"You haven't been on a horse since then?" he asked, surprised.

"I mean I have. Cliff—" She stopped suddenly.

Darnell glanced over at her and could practically feel the tension radiating off her. She held her bag's straps clutched in her hands tight. She glanced down and must have seen how hard she was holding on to her bag.

She let it go and sighed. "Let's just say it's been about a year and a half."

Darnell didn't know who Cliff was, but he was certain he was the reason Natoya was guarded. He wasn't going to push her and ask who he was. It was obvious it was someone she didn't want to speak about.

"Well, then you will be fine. Mavis will be perfect for you. She's one of the smartest mares that we have and she's a gentle soul," he said. He had figured he would need a horse that would be gentle-natured and wouldn't need much instruction.

They drove in a comfortable silence for a little while. The music was low and on one of the country stations. Darnell tapped his finger to the song playing while he focused on the drive. It wasn't going to take long to get to the ranch.

"Have you lived in Shady Springs all of your life?" Natoya's voice cut through the air.

"Born and raised." He grinned.

He loved their town and shared with her how he and his brother had grown up there. They'd had a loving childhood, and Darnell couldn't see raising his children anywhere else but Shady Springs. He glanced over at her and found her listening to him with a small smile on her lips. She laughed when he shared a crazy story of him and Dane getting in trouble around Halloween when they had egged Old Man Saunters' house.

"Wait. What?" She laughed.

Darnell shrugged. It hadn't just been him and his brother. About half the football team been in on it. Mr. Saunters was an old man who hated everyone who was under the age of sixty. The old man had complained about homecoming parade and that the town shouldn't have one.

That the kids who played sports should be focused on schoolwork and not celebrating a game.

So, the football team had snuck onto his property and egged his house. Of course, they had been caught, and their parents hadn't been too happy to pick him and Dane up at the sheriff's department.

"Those were the days." He chuckled. He had plenty of stories he could share with her. He and his brother had always been into something. He eyed her and tapped her on her knee. "Where did you grow up?"

"I grew up outside of Fort Collins," she replied. She shook her head and motioned to him. "But it sounds like my life was boring compared to yours."

She did share some things about her family and friends. She was an only child, was close to her parents, and had a best friend who she was neglecting. It seemed as if she missed her something fierce, but he just couldn't figure out why she was here in Shady Springs. If she was close to her family and friends, had a great job before coming here, then why the move?

"You should have your Emme come down. I'm sure we can take her around town and have some fun," he offered. Anything to help her feel comfortable around him and want to spend more time with him. Even though they were in a small town, there was always something to do.

"She'd like that. She already was looking into it. I need to do some painting and decorating, and she was going to come down to help," she said.

"Let me know if you need help. Painting is one of my other specialties," he said.

She eyed him with one of her eyebrows arched. "Really?"

"No, but I've painted plenty." He chuckled.

"Well, maybe I will take you up on the offer." Her lips curled up into a small smile.

Darnell's heart skipped a beat. Maybe him chipping at her walls was causing a crack. It would only be a matter of time now. The rest of time was spent with them sharing stories with each other. Darnell appreciated the drive to the ranch. It allowed him to see a little more into Natoya, and it just made him want her even more.

"This is beautiful," Natoya said.

They paused the horses at the top of a small slope. Before them were the rolling lands of the Blazing Eagle Ranch. The Brooks family was certainly lucky to own such a beautiful spread. It helped that this was something Darnell saw every day at work. He almost took it for granted, but when he came to this area, it reminded him of the beauty of nature that surrounded them.

There were times when he was in the corral with the horses or out helping with the cattle that he didn't see this side of the property. But there were days where he and Benji spent hours discovering all there was to the ranch. The Brooks family didn't mind their employees on their land on their off hours. A lot of them boarded their horses there.

But right now, even with the acres of gorgeous land before them, Darnell couldn't tear his eyes off Natoya. Her beauty captivated him and took his breath away. She had been a natural getting up on Mavis. She hadn't needed much help. Even though she'd said it'd been a while, she'd got up on Mavis as if she had been doing it daily.

Mavis had been a perfect choice for Natoya, as he had thought. The mare had taken to her immediately. She had nuzzled and greeted her as soon as Natoya got close to her. Even Benji had demanded attention from Natoya. His horse had certainly remembered her by the way he'd trotted to her and wanted a few neck and nose scratches.

"It is," he murmured.

Her gaze cut to his, and she lowered her head immediately with a small smile appearing on her lips. She looked back over at him. He wasn't going to apologize for saying she was beautiful. She was.

"I meant the scenery," she said.

"I know." He glanced around and figured this would be a great spot for them to have their lunch. They had ridden for about an hour. He dismounted from Benji and went over to assist Natoya.

His hands went to her waist, and he helped lift her from the saddle. She slid down the front of him, and he bit back a groan. His cock was already pressing against his jeans. He just hoped she hadn't felt anything, but going by her eyes widening and meeting his, he knew she had. He cleared his throat and released her.

"Thanks," Natoya murmured.

He had yet to back away from her. He should put some room between them, but he couldn't get his feet to move. Her big brown eyes had yet to break their hold on him.

"And for bringing me here. This is better than what I had planned for the day."

"No problem. Anytime you want to ride, just let me know." He cleared his throat and decided he should move before he did something drastic like toss her over his shoulder and carry her over to the tree. He spun on his heel and strode back to Benji. He grabbed their lunches and a blanket from his saddlebags. He held his hand out to Natoya. "Come."

"Are they gonna be okay here?" she asked.

"Of course. They're trained. They won't go far with their grazing." He waited to see if she would slip her hand in his.

She went over to him and slid her hand in his. A feeling unlike any he'd ever known rippled through his chest. They walked over to a large tree that would give them plenty of shade while they enjoyed their lunch.

"I hope you're okay with cold-cut sandwiches and chips," he said.

"I'm famished right now so I would eat my shoe if I had to." She chuckled.

Darnell grinned and was happy that he had packed an extra sandwich for the both of them along with fruits, chips, and some cookies. He had a large appetite and could probably put it all away if he was hungry enough. They arrived at the tree, and he hated he had to let her hand go.

He spread the blanket out for them and motioned for her to take a seat. He sat next to her and placed the one saddlebag that held the food on the blanket in front of them.

"You packed enough food for a small army." Natoya giggled.

He grinned and loved the sound. He made a mental note to do whatever he needed to keep her laughing and smiling. He hadn't liked her shutting down in the truck when the Cliff person was mentioned. This was how he liked to see her. Carefree and happy. He handed her a sandwich. It was bigger than her hand. Maybe he had gone above and beyond when it came to making their lunch.

"Well, I wasn't sure, so I'd rather come with more than not enough," he muttered playfully.

She giggled again and began unwrapping the sandwich. They sat in silence, taking in the scenery while they enjoyed their food. Darnell hadn't realized how hungry he was. He hadn't eaten breakfast on account of him preparing for their friendly ride.

"This is good," she said around her bites. She was halfway through her sandwich. She popped a few chips in her mouth.

"Thanks." There was something about feeding a woman that just sat right with him. Just looking at Natoya gave him the feelings that he needed to take care of her. He knew she didn't need him to actually take care of her, but just the thought that he could do something as simple as feed her appeased something in him.

"You are so lucky. You get to see all this every day when you come to work." She sighed.

"Not all the time. Ranching is not glamorous." He grimaced.

There were plenty of television shows out there that made it seem as if it was an easy job. It was far from it. Some days he went home sore and dead tired. Hell, that was why some of the hands used the ranch house. Sometimes they were too damn tired to drive home only to have to come back bright and early the next morning.

"Oh, I know. But it must help to see this scenery, though. It's so beautiful. Untouched nature. All I get at work is four walls and moody preteenagers and their smells." She laughed.

Yeah, maybe he had the better deal. He didn't know if he could deal with teaching kids.

Some of them tested their parents; he was sure they misbehaved in the classroom. They continued eating their meal. Off in the distance, there was a hawk circling around in the sky. He nudged Natoya with his elbow and pointed to the bird.

"Oh, wow. What is that? A hawk?" She gasped.

"Yeah. Something is either dead out there or about to be." He chuckled.

They sat in silence as they watched nature unfold before their eyes. The hawk swooped in and snatched a small animal from the tall grass. Natoya's gasp met his ears. He turned to find her eyes locked in on the hawk as it flew away from them.

"I know it's nature and we have to let it be, but damn do I want to go and save whatever it caught." She turned to him and shrugged.

The woman had a big heart. He'd seen it with how she'd acted with her students, the way she'd taken her time making sure an older gentleman moved with the song she'd been teaching, and even the patience she'd exuded with him in her class.

How was she single?

Not for long she won't be, a voice whispered in

the back of his head. He agreed. He was going to do whatever he had to do to claim her.

"It'll be okay." He reached out and rested a hand on hers.

She smiled at him, and his heart stuttered again. She had a smudge of mayo on the corner of her mouth. He unconsciously reached up and gently wiped it off. Her tempting lips were soft and plump. He couldn't take his eyes off them. He found himself leaning forward. He paused just a hairsbreadth from her and inhaled her wonderful scent. For a brief moment, he had a fleeting thought that he shouldn't be doing this, but he pushed it down.

He wanted to kiss her.

Needed to.

He lowered his head the rest of the way and touched his lips to hers.

7

atoya wasn't shocked when Darnell's lips touched hers. She had been wondering how long it would take for him to kiss her. She had been thinking of it from the moment he had picked her up from her house. The t-shirt, jeans, boots—it all did something to her.

She had a type, and she was not going to be able to change that. As much as Cliff had fucked her over, she was drawn to Darnell. It was quite obvious that the two men were different.

At least from what she could tell at the moment. In the back of her mind, she was waiting for Darnell to show his true colors, but so far, he just seemed liked a nice guy who had a love for his family, horses, and nature.

Natoya sighed and leaned into the kiss. She parted her lips to allow his tongue to sweep in. It was everything she would have thought from Darnell. His lips moved against hers in a soft motion while his tongue boldly entered her mouth. She raised her hands to rest them on his solid chest. The man was built solidly from hard work on a ranch.

The kiss deepened, and Natoya didn't have any objections. It had been too long since she'd been held by a member of the opposite sex. She had stayed to herself after leaving Cliff. She had just wanted to be by herself. As much as she'd tried to fight this attraction to Darnell, she had come to the hard realization that she was going to be unable to resist him.

So why not take advantage of the situation?

Was it wrong for her to be selfish and indulge in a man who obviously wanted her? She didn't know if it was wrong, but right now, being in Darnell's arms felt right. She moved closer to him with her arms coming around his neck. He lifted her as if she weighed nothing and brought her to straddle him.

Their lips had yet to separate.

Natoya moaned at the feel of his large hands

cupping her ass. She wiggled on his lap and felt his stiff member underneath her.

"Natoya." Darnell tore his mouth from hers. He cupped her cheek and stared into her eyes. His dark-brown ones were lit with a fire that burned.

Just for her.

When was the last time someone had looked at her like that? It made her feel needed, sexy, and beautiful.

"What?" she murmured.

Her gaze trailed down to his lips and to his chest that was rising and falling fast. She needed to see him without his shirt. She could feel the ridges of his abdomen. Her fingertips ghosted his chest and stomach until she reached the edge of his shirt. She grabbed it and pulled it over his head. She tossed it somewhere behind him. Her eyes took him all in, and just like she'd thought, he was chiseled perfectly, and these were no gym muscles. This was a man who had worked hard on a ranch and earned every ridge on his abdomen. Her fingers found their way to the center of his chest.

"Are you sure?" he rasped.

Her gaze flicked to his. She jerked her head in a nod. There was no way she was walking away.

She rocked her hips and felt him underneath her. It drew a low moan from her. He was large, and she wanted to see his dick.

Natoya didn't wait for him to reach for her shirt. She tugged it over her head and tossed it over to where his was. The warmth from the sun kissed her skin. She smiled at the look that crossed his face. Darnell's eyes had dropped down to her breasts that were encased in her black lace bra. The hunger that blazed in his dark eyes had her stoking the need that burned inside her.

He brought her back flush to him and took her lips in another kiss. This time it was harder and dominating. His tongue stroked hers in a sensual dance. Another moan slipped from her. Darnell's hand slid around to her back, and he undid the clasp of her bra. She wiggled out of it and moved it out of the way. He tore his lips from hers and reached for her. His large hands cupped her breast. She held on to his shoulders and allowed her head to fall back, and he tasted her mounds. His lips closed around her perky nipples that were drawn into tight buds.

Natoya inched her fingers up his neck and dove them into his thick hair. She entwined her fingers into his locks and held on. He nipped her, drawing a cry from her. She tightened her hold on his hair while she rotated her hips, teasing herself and him. Her core pulsed with need. She needed to feel him inside her.

Darnell's warm hands coasted around to her back to hold her in place while he focused on suckling and kissing on her breasts. The whirlwind sensation inside her was building. Her eyes were closed as she basked in the feelings that rocked through her.

"Darnell," she whispered.

She opened her eyes slightly, leaned forward, and placed her lips on his. He must have seen something in her eyes. He released a curse and flipped them over to where she landed on her back. The blanket had been placed over a soft, thick bed of grass. They worked together to remove her jeans, leaving her in only her panties. Darnell stood and hopped out of his jeans and left his boxer briefs on. There was a large tent from his cock pushing against the material. She swallowed hard at the size of him. She had felt that he may be large, but she hadn't thought that size.

He came back to her and lay next to her. He leaned over her and brushed her hair from her face.

"Natoya, I really do like you," he said.

He studied her, and it was then she felt as if she were the most beautiful woman in the world. The gentle way he glided his fingers down the center of her chest had her whimpering.

"Mm-hmm." She bit her lip to keep from admitting that he she really liked him, too. She didn't want to put herself out there at the moment. She didn't want to risk getting hurt. Right now, she just wanted to feel.

Darnell's lips ghosted her cheeks and moved down to her neck. She arched her face away and allowed him to access the column of her neck. He continued on a journey to her chest where he massaged and paid such focused attention to her breasts. She sighed as he took his time bathing her nipples with his tongue and suckling her.

Her fingers found their way back to his hair while he moved farther down her. His tongue swept along her stomach. She bit back a moan, the sensation of him licking her sending a thrill through her down to her core.

He moved between her legs while she spread them open for him. She lifted, and he slipped her panties down her legs and tossed them over onto the blanket. He inhaled sharply and focused on her center. She combed his hair with her fingers and watched him explore her. His finger dove between her folds and met her slick wetness. Her core clenched with anticipation.

"Jesus, Natoya," he breathed.

The look of wonder in his eyes had her breath catching in her throat. He leaned down and captured her clit with his lips, and her eyes rolled back. Her body jerked from his full-out assault on her swollen bundle of nerves.

"Darnell," she gasped.

He rolled and teased her clit with such expertise that promised she would reach her peak soon. She fisted his hair, and he took her to greater heights. Everything was overwhelming. He consumed her with his all. A tingling sensation started from the tops of her head and rippled all the way to her toes. Her body ached, needing everything that his mouth and tongue promised.

The man certainly knew what he was doing. Natoya trembled from the feeling of his finger circling her entrance. He pushed one inside her, eliciting a moan from her. He thrust it deep before adding another one. His other hand crept up and captured her breast. Her head fell back onto the blanket, and she turned herself over to the pleasure that coursed through her.

He worked her body so well that she felt as if

she were truly floating toward the sky. His hands, his tongue, and even the sound of his moans drove her insane. Her hips gyrated of their own accord in rhythm with his hand.

"Darnell," she cried out his name this time. She released his hair and was unsure what to hold on to. She gripped his shoulders, digging her nails into his warm skin. The pleasure was mounting in her. Natoya made one mistake.

She glanced down and found his heated gaze on her.

Her body detonated.

She arched off the blanket. His steady hands held her down. Her body trembled with a fierceness as he drew every ounce of pleasure from her.

She came down from her climax and rested back down on the blanket. Her arms and legs felt heavy. He withdrew his fingers from her, but his tongue lazily continued to lick her. Unable to move, she basked in the aftershocks of her climax. She finally was able to open her eyes.

"Natoya," Darnell rasped.

She blinked to clear her vision and found his eyes filled with an intense passion and desire.

"Please." It was the only words she could formulate. It was easy to see what he was asking, and there was no doubt in her answering.

He pushed up and took off his shorts before he crawled over her. He rested himself on his elbows to keep the majority of his weight off her. He was solid muscle, and she wanted to feel him on her. She reached for him and pulled his head down toward hers to offer her lips. He crushed his to hers. She opened immediately and teased his tongue with hers. She tasted herself on his tongue. Her desire for this man grew even more.

She shifted her legs and rested her knees on his waist. She was impatient and needed him inside her. He reached between them without breaking their kiss to line his cock up with her opening.

He trailed hot kisses along her cheek and nuzzled his face in the crook of his neck. He thrust once and sent his cock deep. A cry tore from her and echoed through the air at the thick invasion. Her breath was ripped from her lungs, her body stretching to accommodate him. He paused and held still.

Natoya gasped and tried to draw in air again. She wrapped her arms around him. He was a large man, and her body took a few moments to adapt to his girth. She blinked and found him watching her.

"You're so fucking tight," he murmured.

She squeezed her inner muscles, testing out her core. Her muscles were stretched to full capacity, and it was one of the best feelings she had experienced. His eyes held a tender concern that made her heart skip a beat.

"Are you okay?"

"Yeah, I'm fine," she whispered. She was more than okay.

He kissed her hard then moved. He withdrew from her slightly then thrust home again. He set a steady pace that she didn't hesitate to meet. Her body arched to meet his, and they writhed in rhythm together.

Nothing else existed besides them.

Natoya didn't want this moment to ever end. Darnell's pace quickened, sending his cock completely inside her. He reached down and held on to her thigh. He brought it up higher, the angle of his cock hitting differently. Cries escaped her. She couldn't—wouldn't—hold back.

The pleasure was mounting, becoming too much for her. Her core clenched around him. Her body was strung tight from the emotions swirling around inside her. His muscles grew taut underneath her fingertips. His gasps and groans joined her cries.

He thrust harder as if he wanted to claim her.

Her cries turned into pants. Her skin was slick with perspiration from their lovemaking. She couldn't get enough of him.

And that thought was dangerous.

Their eyes met. Something was there between them. It would be hard to deny that they had chemistry.

"Darnell," she whimpered.

She was so damn close to reaching another climax that she was in awe of the man drawing it from her. Darnell's movements became frantic and urgent. He lifted her other leg and rested his palms on the backs of her thighs to change their position. He pounded into her, his grunts filling her ears. The slap of flesh could be heard, and it only fueled Natoya's desire to reach her peak.

Natoya fell over into oblivion, her second orgasm crashing into her. She cried out, her body trembling and shaking. The sensation of Darnell's dick inside her drew out the climax. It was hard and took her breath away.

"Natoya!" Darnell roared.

He tensed and grew still as he emptied himself into her. She opened her eyes and watched him throw his head back while he held himself still. His cock pulsed inside her, ropes of his seed filling her.

He was magnificent.

Natoya couldn't tear her gaze away from him. He fell forward and caught himself from crashing down on her. Her legs fell to the side and rested along his thighs. She wrapped her arms around him, needing to feel his warm body on top of hers.

"I'm too heavy," he muttered.

"Don't move. I like the feeling of you on me," she whispered.

Hell, at the moment, she didn't want to let him go. Even with his cock at half-mast inside her, it felt damn good. Her gaze shifted to over his shoulder to the big, open Colorado sky.

She didn't want this moment to ever end.

"I SWEAR I DIDN'T BRING YOU UP HERE FOR this," Darnell's deep voice rumbled near her ear.

Natoya smiled and felt his arms tighten around her. After their world-shattering love-making, he had put on his boxers and jeans while she was semi dressed. She had thrown on her shirt and panties. Realization had dawned on her as they had lain there basking in their postcoitus state out under the sky. Darnell had laughed at her horror that she'd had sex out in the open where who knew could have seen them.

He pulled her back to where her back rested along his chest. Her head was cradled by his arm as they lay together taking in the beautiful scenery. Natoya thought she would have felt ashamed or embarrassed due to sleeping with Darnell on their first date—outing—together, but she didn't.

This was not supposed to be a date, but just him taking her riding as a friend. Someone to get to know. She rolled over and was met with his bare chest. There was a light sprinkling of hair along his stomach that led beneath his shorts. She leaned forward and pressed her nose against him. She missed having a warm male body near her who wanted her by him. It had been entirely too long, and maybe that was why she'd reacted to Darnell so strongly.

She just needed to be fucked thoroughly, and he had definitely excelled at the job.

He tilted her chin upward to meet his eyes. There was a twinkle in them that had her face warming. She was busted at ogling him. His brown eyes drew her in. There were minute flecks of gold in them that intrigued her. He studied her and waited for her to respond.

"I'm sure you didn't," she replied. She snuggled closer to him, loving the feel of his hardness against her softness. Not even a blade of grass could fit between them. She closed her eyes and basked in the warmth of him at her front and the sun at her back. Darnell's scent was that of nature, sandalwood, and musk. She breathed him in and tried to commit it to memory.

"This may be too late, but why don't I take you out on an official date." His words came out low.

She stiffened at the thought. Was she truly ready to date? She may have had sex with Darnell today, but was she ready to enter into another relationship? He must have felt her tense and tightened his hold on her. He tipped her chin upward again to force her to look at him.

"Just me and you. Nothing crazy. Dinner, a few drinks, then I'll take you home."

Natoya hesitated. Would it hurt to allow him to take her out? They had already slept together. Maybe it was time for her to take a chance. She had needed to protect herself and didn't want to get hurt. In her heart, she knew she wanted a partner and children. But she couldn't have that if she didn't put herself out there.

Even if it was with another cowboy.

Darnell's thumb trailed along her lip as he patiently waited. Had this been Cliff, he would have yelled at her for making him wait. He'd called her names and could get belligerent.

But that wasn't Darnell.

"Okay."

He swooped down and covered her lips with his in a hard kiss. She laughed at his excitement and wrapped her arms around his neck while returning the kiss with the same fervor. At the moment, her heart was screaming she was making the right decision, while her gut hollered a reminder of what she had promised herself.

No more cowboys.

Darnell rolled them over to where he loomed over her. His hand slipped underneath her shirt, and all thoughts went completely out the window. She'd worry about everything later. Right now, she was a little preoccupied.

&ℰ&   8   ℰ&

Natoya jumped in her car and breathed a deep sigh. It was Monday, and it was the Monday of all Mondays in the history of Mondays. The attitudes floated around in the classroom today. She'd had to hand out three referrals to the office. She didn't know what was going on, but to say she was happy that her workday was over was an understatement. She rested back in her chair and just absorbed the quietness of her car.

She inhaled deeply then slowly blew out her breath. She could feel her heart rate begin to lower. She did the exercise again and calmed down slightly. What she needed was a hot shower, a glass—maybe bottle—of wine, and good food.

Secretly, she wished she could go back to two

days ago where she had spent the day in Darnell's arms out in the open under the bluest of skies on the Blazing Eagle Ranch. A smile appeared on her lips at the memory of their time there. The horseback ride had been so much fun, and the lovemaking—sex—was out of this world. She frowned at the thought of calling what they'd done lovemaking. They barely knew each other.

She liked him but doubted she was in love with him. But either way, the chemistry between the two of them was electric. Goosebumps appeared on her skin at the memory of him poised over her, thrusting his long, thick cock into her. She bit her lip and held back a whimper.

"Get a grip, girl," she whispered.

She hit the start button to turn her car on. She eyed the parking lot and saw there were only a few cars that remained. It had been an extremely long day, and she had stayed over to help a few kids. That she hadn't minded. She always made time to help her students who were behind or just needed a better explanation of their lessons. It had been everything else from the unruly students to an unexpected staff meeting to the unexpected fire drill. Apparently, one of the students had thought it would be funny to pull the fire alarm. Thankfully, the student in question was not one of hers.

Tonight, Darnell was going to pick her up and take her out for their official first date. Butterflies filled her stomach. She laughed at the thought of being nervous. Hell, the man had not only already seen her naked but had drawn multiple orgasms from her. It had been a perfect day. They had spent hours out on the ranch. When they had finally decided to leave, he had been right. Benji and Mavis hadn't traveled far.

A sigh escaped her at the memory of their ride back to the barn. He hadn't wanted to let her go, so she rode sidesaddle in front of him on Benji. Mavis had trailed close behind them. The memory of his firm body behind hers, with his arms wrapped around her loosely, had her all up in her feelings.

Was he the one?

She began the drive home. She needed to shower and figure out what she was going to wear. He'd said they would go somewhere simple. Drinks and a bite to eat. She could handle that. Her cellphone's ringer cut through the air. She hit the connect button on her steering wheel to allow it to go through to her car's hands-free system. It was Emme calling.

"Hey, girl," she greeted her best friend.

A smile slipped in place as she thought about the updates she had to give her. Emme and Natoya shared everything with each other. Emme knew all of Natoya's ups and downs. Even everything with Cliff. She had been a big supporter of Natoya relocating to get away from him and start over.

"You're not still at the school, are you?" Emme asked. Her friend knew her so well. Even being in different parts of the state, Emme knew that Natoya was a dedicated teacher and stayed afterward plenty of days.

"No, but I did just leave. I'm on my way home." She glanced over at her watch and hadn't realized it was a little later than normal, though. She had a few hours before Darnell would be picking her up. "What's up?"

"So it looks like I can take a long weekend this weekend. Why don't I drive down Thursday night after work and stay the weekend? My boss gave me Friday and Monday off if I want it," Emme announced.

"That would be perfect," Natoya exclaimed. It would be good to see her longtime friend. She immediately began thinking of what they could do. Yes, they would work on painting like she wanted to do, but they needed to have girl time together and just catch up with each other in person. There was nothing like having a girls' day with the bestie. "I'll see if they can get a substitute to cover me on Friday and Monday. That way I will be all yours for four days."

Natoya gripped the steering wheel, dying to mention Darnell. She guided her car through town, barely seeing the scenery. In the year since she had moved to Shady Springs, this drive home from work was automatic.

"Good...and what's up with you? Your voice sounds different." It was amazing how Emme had detected a change in Natoya.

Her friend couldn't even see her and she recognized something in just the tone of Natoya's voice. The woman had a way about her when it came to people. She could sense a lie before a person even spoke. When Natoya had first started dating Cliff, it had been Emme who had warned her. She hadn't liked him, but she'd tolerated him at first only because Natoya had been in a relationship with him.

Natoya, blind to the red flags that he'd exuded, thought she was in love. He was nice. He was sexy. He had been the man she'd thought she wanted.

She had been so wrong.

It wasn't until months after they had been together that he began to show his true colors. His aggressiveness, possessiveness, and narcissistic behaviors. She remembered the first night she had a peek into who he truly was. They had been out grabbing a drink. She'd gone with him and a couple of his friends. A guy had apparently been looking at her and trying to get her attention. She had been oblivious to it. She was having fun and had one or two drinks in her system.

Cliff hadn't appreciated it. He and his friends went over and roughed the poor guy up. The fight had gotten out of control with the police being called. Natoya hadn't known what the brawl had been for until Cliff had dragged the guy over to her.

"This is the last time you look at her. She's mine," Cliff had sneered.

His friends laughed and high-fived each other. Natoya stared in horror at the poor guy. His eyes had already begun to swell from the punches that had landed.

She blinked and shook off the memory. The police had come and hadn't arrested Cliff and his friends. No, they'd served tickets.

That was the start of many incidents.

"What? I don't know what you're talking about." Natoya chuckled. She coasted to a halt at one of the few stop lights in town. It was an intersection in downtown that did get a little busy at this time of day when most of the towns-people were getting off work and were on their way home. She rolled down the window halfway and breathed in the fresh air. The sun was large and beautiful and should be setting soon. The warm air filled her car. She turned off the air-conditioning to allow the warmth to pour into the vehicle.

"I know you, and you're hiding something." Her suspicious friend was not going to let go.

Natoya suddenly felt shy. She hadn't spoken to anyone about Darnell, and she really didn't have close friends yet in Shady Springs. At least none that she could share the personal details with, such as what had transpired between her and Darnell.

"Bitch, you know I love you, right?"

"Out with it!" Emme giggled. The excitement that filled her voice was almost palpable.

Natoya grinned at her friend's squeal.

"I knew it," Emme said. "Something's happened since the last time we spoke."

"Yeah. It did. I, um, sort of met someone," Natoya admitted.

Emme squealed again, and Natoya could envision her friend jumping up and down.

"What do you mean, sort of? Tell me all about it. Who is he? What does he look like? Does he have a big dick and a single brother?"

Natoya's grin widened. She drove through the light and continued on her journey home. Of course Emme would ask these very important questions that a best friend would want to know.

"Emerson!" Natoya laughed. She arrived at her street and made the turn. Seeing the home she had purchased with her hard work come into view made her heart speed up.

Or was it thoughts of Darnell?

She turned into her driveway and parked in front of her garage. She still had a lot of boxes stored in there until she could finish arranging her house to the way she wanted it. Luckily enough, Shady Springs was relatively safe, and she didn't have any concerns about leaving her car parked outside.

She killed the engine and sat and stared at her home. She was so damn proud of herself.

"Oh, yeah. He must have a big dick," Emme murmured.

"Well, his name is Darnell. He is so damn sexy." Natoya sighed thinking of his brown eyes, his smile, and his soft kisses. Her friend was crazy, and that was why she loved her so much. "He does have a brother who I believe is single. And why would you assume that I know his dick size already?"

Emme fell into a fit of laughter. Natoya grabbed her work bag from the passenger seat and her phone. It disconnected from the car's speakers and switched over to itself. She got out of the car and headed into the house. She beelined it to her bedroom so that she could start to get ready. After the day she'd had, she deserved a long, hot shower or maybe even a soak in the tub.

"See, the way you said his name led me to believe that you do know the size of his dick," Emme declared.

Natoya rolled her eyes at her friend's silly way of coming to a conclusion about the size of Darnell's dick. She tossed her bag down and kicked her shoes off. She was not going to share the size of his dick with her friend.

For once, this seemed too personal. In the past she may have, but with Darnell it was none of her friend's business that he'd stretched her out like no other. Her core clenched with the memory of his intimate invasion into her. She put her phone on her nightstand and hit the button for the speakerphone.

"Anywho, we are changing the subject," Natoya said.

"Oh, no we are not. Where did you meet this Darnell? What does he do for a living?"

Emme was so damn persistent, but Natoya understood why. Her friend had been by her side for years and knew her history with men.

"Well, actually, I met him at my job. He was helping with the field day event they had," she said. She began stripping her clothes off. Who would have thought she would have met a guy at her job? Most of the teachers who worked at the school were either older, or too young, or were married. "And, um, he works on a ranch here."

"I thought you said you were avoiding men like Cliff?" Emme asked quietly.

Natoya cringed at the sudden seriousness in the tone of her voice. She blew out a deep breath and carried her clothes over to her basket in the foot of her closet. Of course her friend wouldn't hold back any punches.

Yeah, she had said that. No more men who worked on ranches, farms, wore a cowboy hat or even the damn boots. She had been tired of them all.

She walked back over and scooped her phone up and went into her bathroom.

"I know, but Darnell isn't anything like Cliff," she replied. Not that she knew him well. It didn't take much to have sex with a person. Not that she ever judged people for sleeping together on their first dates. As long as both parties were of age and consented, they could have all the fun they wanted.

And that was what she'd done with Darnell. There had been no regrets when they'd parted. If anything, she was already excited to see him again.

Just because they'd slept together didn't mean that they were committed to each other. They'd had a grown-up and sexy afternoon together, and now he was wanting to take her out. No attachments. He was welcome to do as he pleased, just as she was.

A frown formed. She honestly didn't like the idea of him with another woman. He didn't give her the sense that he was a playboy and hopped around between women. She rested a hand on her belly, a funny sensation floating through her. Was that jealousy? She had never had this feeling before. Even when she had found out that Cliff had been cheating on her, she hadn't felt the need to do someone bodily harm. She just wanted to walk away from him, but he wouldn't let her.

He'd kept pulling her back in, and she'd kept falling for it.

He'd promise that was the last time. He'd been drunk. It wasn't his fault.

All excuses she knew better than to accept, but she just didn't leave. He'd demand that she get over it and move on. There had been so many damn red flags that she'd ignored. That they were good for each other.

But now she knew better.

"How do you know? We all thought Cliff was a good guy. A little crazy, but hell, who isn't, and look where that got you. Far from me because of him," Emme said.

Natoya winced. Her friend was laying it on the line.

Natoya turned on the shower, deciding she'd just jump in and wash herself since she still had to decide on what she was going to wear. She placed her hand in the stream of water to test it out. It was a little cool still.

"Well, damn. Tell me how you really feel," Natoya said. She was going to wait a few more minutes to give the water time to warm up a bit. She liked it to be hot so it could melt the stress out of her muscles.

"You know I'm going to be one hundred percent honest with you, babe." Emme's voice softened.

Natoya had to suddenly fight back tears. She would expect no less from Emme and appreciated her friend more than she would ever know. It had been Emme listening to her when she'd complained about Cliff's treatment of her. It had been Emme who had helped move her shit from his place and into her parents' home. It had even been Emme who had helped her look for new jobs and homes away from the town she'd grown up in. Emme knew her better than anyone else.

"That's why I love you," Natoya whispered. One fat tear fell from her eye and slid down her cheek. She sniffed and wiped it away.

"Oh, no crying now. We've done enough of that."

"I'm not."

"I know you. You are a big ol' sap and will cry at the drop of a hat."

"Whatever." That got Natoya to smile. She was a big crybaby. She could be reading a book with a sad passage and she'd be tearing up, or a sad part in a movie and she'd have tears in her eyes. She chuckled and desperately missed her friend. "So you promise you're coming this weekend?"

"Wild horses couldn't hold me back. I hope I get to meet this Darnell."

"Of course. Maybe we can all go out to lunch or something so you can meet him," Natoya said.

If anyone needed to meet him, it would be Emme. She had a sense about people, and after the last debacle in Natoya's relationship with Cliff, she would appreciate Emme's insight into Darnell.

Last time she hadn't listened. This time she would be all ears.

9

Darnell killed the engine and stared at Natoya's home. Why he was nervous, he didn't know. She'd been on his mind every moment since their day together. Now here they were, about to go out for the first time. Even though they had put the cart before the horse, everything would be fine. He ran a hand along his face and tried to will his racing heart to slow down.

He exited the vehicle and made his way to her front door. He pushed the doorbell and waited. It didn't take long for her to answer. His breath caught in his throat at the sight of her. He'd told her they would go to his favorite bar for food and drinks. The Tipsy Cow was a popular hangout spot in Shady Springs, and they really did have great food. If he was going to help Natoya get to know the town and him, then he'd take her somewhere everyone went.

She stepped out of the house dressed in jeans that molded to her curves. She locked up the house. His eyes dropped down to her ass. He'd come to know those curvy hips and plump backside. Her shirt revealed both of her sexy shoulders. She turned back to him with a sensual smile. Her makeup and jewelry were all simple and perfect. Natoya was a natural beauty and didn't need it. He stared at her feet and swallowed hard. She had on heels that gave her a few inches of height. She was still shorter than him, but they certainly gave her a sex appeal that had him wanting to toss her over his shoulder and carry her back into her home.

"Am I dressed okay?" Her husky voice broke through his thoughts.

"Yeah." He had to clear his throat that had gone completely dry.

His gaze moved back up and met hers. There was a twinkle in her eye that brought a flush up his face. It was amazing how just looking at her brought out certain possessive feelings inside him. He had said he'd take it slow with her, but damn, did he just want to go from zero to sixty. He wanted to claim this woman as his.

But something held him back.

The look in her eyes when they'd first met.

"You are beautiful," he murmured. He reached for her hand and brought her forward. He softly kissed her lips and had to restrain himself.

She entwined their fingers together and smiled.

"Thank you." She lifted her purse strap higher onto her shoulder. Her head tilted to the side. "Are we going or are we just going to stand here on my porch?"

"Yeah." He barked a laugh. He motioned toward his truck. What the hell was he doing? He was standing there like a lovesick teenager. He escorted her to his vehicle and helped her inside. Once he was sure she had her safety belt on, he jogged over to his side and got in. The scent of her perfume had taken over the cab. He inhaled it and remembered it from the other day. He didn't know what it was, but it fit her perfectly. "Are you hungry?"

"I'm famished." She laughed.

He loved the sound of it and smiled. He pulled the truck out of her driveway and began the ride to the bar. It wasn't going to take them long to get there. He turned down the music so they could talk.

"Good. The Tipsy Cow has the best burgers and wings in town," he said.

"I've heard of that place, but I've never been," Natoya said.

She turned slightly to face him. The sun had just gone down, but the sky hadn't darkened all the way to night yet. She watched him as he drove. He pulled his hat off and tossed it in the backseat.

"You go there often?" she asked.

"Yeah. My friends and I usually hang out there after work on Fridays if we're not too tired. Usually we'll grab a bite, a few drinks, or to go watch a game after a long day," he admitted. He was a frequent flyer at the Tipsy Cow. Everyone pretty much knew him there. "You'll like it. They play some good music."

"Sounds nice."

He began offering up other places in Shady Springs that he thought she'd like. Even though it was a small town, there was plenty to do. That was why he loved it so much. Most people would think that small towns had nothing to do and were just farming communities, but Shady Springs was so much more than that.

"I've been here a year and I still don't feel like I know the place." Natoya laughed. She reached up and tucked her dark hair behind her ear.

Darnell didn't think she knew how sexy the move was. He wanted to lean forward and nibble on her earlobe then nuzzle his face into the crook of her neck. He pushed down those thoughts, because they were quite dangerous. His cock twitched at the thought. He bit back a groan and tried to will his damn dick to behave.

"I must need to get out more," she said.

"If you want, I can introduce you around," he offered.

He was sure Maddy and the girls would include her in their circle. He gripped the steering wheel tight. But how would he introduce her to them? His girlfriend? They weren't there yet. His friend? He didn't like the sound of that. They had crossed that line out on the Blazing Eagle.

"That would be nice. This may sound sad, but I don't really have friends here. I am cool with some of my coworkers, but ever since moving here, I've just stayed to myself."

He glanced over at her. He didn't know how it would feel to uproot from his home and move to an entirely different town or city and not know anyone.

"It's not sad. I'm sure there was a good reason for you to move here. It takes time, and hell, you hadn't met me yet." He grinned, trying to make light of the situation.

She laughed and shook her head.

"No, I hadn't met you yet. That's what I needed. Darnell in my life." She batted her eyelashes dramatically. Her smile widened as she fell into a fit of giggles.

"Damn right, you needed me," he playfully growled.

He reached over, unable to resist touching her. He grabbed her knee and gave it a slight squeeze. She just didn't know what she was in store for. This was a beautiful woman, and he wanted her. She reached down and covered his hand with hers. He flipped it over and entwined their fingers again. It felt as natural as breathing to hold her hand. She glanced over at him and offered him a small smile.

He coasted the truck to a stop at the red light. They were a few minutes from the bar. He raised her hand and brought it to his lips. He kissed the back of her hand. Her lips parted slightly as she watched him. The urge to lean over and capture them was strong.

A horn blared behind them.

The light had turned green. He kept hold of her hand and turned back to focus on the road. He drove with his one hand. She tightened her hold on him, and he loved the feeling of her smaller hand in his.

"These people you will be introducing me to, who are they?" she asked.

He chuckled and thought of the girls. They would love her. He'd heard nothing but praise from some of them since the line dancing class. They were already talking about going back.

"Well, you've met some of them already. The women who were with me at the class," he said.

He shared with her their compliments of her and the class. They were even more determined to force their significant others to join in and go.

"I'm glad they enjoyed themselves. I at first thought you were involved with one of them," she said.

"Hell no." He'd had a feeling she had been hurt by someone in the past. Someone who may not have been faithful. Hell, he knew all about that. The shit that Melanie had pulled had hurt, and the way she'd done it and her words. He tried not to bring up the memories of how people had treated him afterward. He hated to see the pity in their expressions. Even to this day, he still caught the same look, but he ignored it as best he could. "When I'm with you, I'm with you and only you."

He gave a squeeze to her hand and glanced over at her. There was a weird expression that passed briefly on her face. That let him know everything he needed to know.

Yeah, some dipshit had cheated on her.

How or why? Darnell couldn't even fathom why. Natoya was beautiful, intelligent, funny, and sexy. He may not have known her long, but what he did know had him scrambling to make her his.

"I'm sorry," she said.

"There's nothing to be sorry about, but I can see how you came to that conclusion. A guy attending a class with women who he's cool with. I guess anyone would have assumed it, too, but I promise you, all of them are happily committed to my friends and coworkers. They just talked me into coming with them," he admitted.

He drew into the lot of the Tipsy Cow. Even though it was a weekday, it was almost full. Many people took advantage of the good food and stopped to get a bite to eat after work. Even Darnell was guilty of grabbing his food to go when he didn't feel like cooking anything once he got home.

"Wow. There's a lot of people here on a Monday," Natoya murmured.

She glanced around as he tried to find them a spot to park. He finally found one in the middle where someone had just pulled out. He snagged it before anyone else could. He threw the truck in park and killed the engine.

"I told you they had good food, and they don't water down their drinks either," he said.

He couldn't take his eyes off her. He reached in the back and snagged his wide-brimmed hat. It was a dark one that his mother had bought him last Christmas. Today felt like a good day to bring it out instead of a dusty one he wore for work. He had thrown on a freshly starched button-down shirt, jeans, and his favorite boots. He'd even say he looked damn good.

He stepped out of the vehicle and headed to her door where she waited. He opened it and held out a hand for her. She slid hers into his and allowed him to help her down from the cab. He moved her gently to the side and shut the door. She stared up at him, and his resistance was shattered. He pushed the brim of his hat back and leaned down and covered her lips with his.

Those soft, plump lips immediately opened for him. The kiss rocked him and took his breath away. She leaned forward into him, her fingers gripping his shirt. She tasted of warm honey and sex. He held her to him while he deepened the kiss. Her tongue stroked his and offered a promise he soon would collect on. He lifted his head slightly and gazed down into her eyes.

"I've been waiting to do that since you stepped out of your house," he admitted. His heart was racing like a wild horse given free rein to run. He was surprised she couldn't hear its thundering beat.

"Same," she whispered. Her lips curved up in a sensual smile.

He growled softly, leaned down, and fused his lips hard to hers for one more taste. He lifted his head and sighed. He'd promised her a night out on the town, not to get mauled by him in the parking lot of a bar. Her lips were already swelling from his kisses. He had to keep from reaching down to adjust his hardened member that was pressing against his jeans.

"Well, pretty lady. Let me take you inside so I can feed you." He chuckled.

They would have a good time tonight. He'd ensure it. After they'd eaten and had some drinks, maybe they could take it a little further and either go back to his place or hers. He didn't care where as long as it ended with the two of them naked in a bed this time.

Not that he hadn't minded having her under the big open Colorado sky. This time, he wanted her in the privacy of a bedroom.

All night.

He took her by the hand and led her toward the Tipsy Cow. They arrived at the door where one of the security guards was posted.

"Darnell." Rob nodded. He reached for the door and held it open for them.

"Hey, Rob. How's the night going?" Darnell asked. He guided Natoya ahead of him so she could enter first.

"Smooth, and it better stay that way." Rob chuckled.

Darnell grinned and bumped Rob's fist with his as he passed through the doorway. Country music blared through the speakers, giving it that small-town bar vibe. Natoya leaned into him while they walked along. He knew to find a table, and a server would be over to them in no time. He led them through the throng of tables until he found a half booth in the back. It was one of his favorites that gave him a full view of the place.

"Thanks," Natoya murmured as he helped her slide into the booth.

He joined her and raised his hand to flag down one of the regular servers.

"Hey, Darnell. You need a menu or you know what y'all want?" Tiffany said when she arrived at the table.

"Can you bring a menu for her, please?" he asked. He already knew what he'd be ordering. He was a simple guy and ordered one of two things when he came.

"Sure. Give me one second." She spun around headed toward the bar.

"What do you get when you come?" Natoya asked.

He grinned and leaned back to rest an arm on the back of the booth. He patted his stomach which was signaling it was time to eat.

"Either their triple bacon cheeseburger and fries, or I get their devil's hot and honey wings with fries."

"Devil's hot and honey? Oh, no. That doesn't even sit right with my stomach." Her eyes widened. She shook her head and laughed. "Why would you want to eat anything with the devil's name in it? That will burn a hole right through your stomach."

"It hasn't so far." He laughed. He did love a good hot wing or anything with hot in front of it. He was a sucker for abuse when it came to eating hot things. He shared a few stories of him trying the hottest wings they had. The Tipsy Cow had an annual contest of who could eat their hottest wings. One year, he and his brother had entered. That night, neither of them had slept. Thankfully, the house they had shared at the time had two bathrooms.

"Oh, my goodness!" Natoya laughed with tears streaming down her face. She reached up to wipe them away.

Tiffany had returned and dropped off the menus. She'd taken their drink orders with the promise to return soon.

Natoya waved a hand in front of her eyes.

"Yeah, that was the last time I tried ghost pepper wings." He snorted. He'd even had to call off work the next day. He grimaced with the memory. The devil's hot and honey, he could handle. They were really good. Tonight, though, he'd play it safe and go with the burger.

Soon they had placed their order and had their drinks. Darnell was enjoying himself immensely. Natoya was opening up about her life and where she'd grown up. She'd even talked about her best friend, Emerson, or Emme for short. Just by the way she spoke of her, he could see how much she missed her and how close they were.

It was almost like him and his brother, Dane. Darnell was five years older, but they were the best of friends growing up and still were.

"You should invite her to come down. We can go out. I can rustle up the gang, and we can have a night out on the town to welcome Emme to Shady Springs," he offered.

He knew he could ask any of the guys to bring their girls along. Hell, even some of the other hands would come out just for a beer. He thought of the new hand, Zach. He definitely needed to come out with them. He was a good worker, quiet, and was former military. He'd even promised Darnell the next time he'd ask he would come with them.

"That sounds fun. I'm sure she would love that. She's already coming. She's supposed to be here on Thursday," Natoya said.

"Well, hell. Then I'll rustle everyone up. I'm sure I can get some people to come out either Friday or Saturday. Did y'all have anything planned?" he asked. He reached for his mug and took a sip out of it. The Tipsy Cow always had the best brew on tap.

"A few things. She's going to help with the painting this weekend, we'll probably go get manis and pedis, plenty of wine...you know, girls' weekend." She reached for her drink and took a sip.

Tiffany arrived at that moment with their food.

Natoya's eyes went wide when she saw the serving size. "Oh my, this looks wonderful. Thank you!"

"You are welcome, my dear. Can I get you anything else?" Tiffany asked. She nodded toward Darnell's almost empty mug. "Want another one?"

"Sure. One more won't hurt," he said. He eyed his burger, and his stomach rumbled. The triple burger was massive, and from experience he knew it was going to be so damn good. The bar utilized the local farmers and butchers to get fresh meats and veggies.

They ate in comfortable silence. The bar was hopping for a Monday night. Darnell saw plenty of people who he knew. A few even stopped over to chat. He'd introduced Natoya to everyone. He bit back labeling her, so she'd just been Natoya.

He had a need to claim her as his woman when the men stopped by. There was a curiosity in their expressions that left him wanting to kill any notion that they had a chance with her.

"You certainly are popular," Natoya said. She licked the sauce from her fingers.

His gaze dropped down to her lips. Once she was done, she reached for her napkin. His burger paused on its way down. He had to force the food down his throat completely. The woman was trying to kill him, and she didn't even know it. She turned her wide eyes on him and tilted her head. Those plump lips of hers curved up in a smile.

"You okay?"

"Yeah." He gave a cough. He reached for his beer to help clear his throat. Choking on a burger would not have been cool. He took a large sip and felt now as if he would be able to speak without tearing up. "I grew up here. My family's been here in Shady Springs for as long as I know."

"That's nice."

A weird expression passed over her face. It didn't take a rocket scientist to know it had to do something with her being in Shady Springs. He would have to help her like it here. There was no way she could leave.

He nodded toward her almost empty plate. "Everything good?"

"Oh my, yes." She leaned back in her chair and patted her stomach.

There was nothing sexier than a woman who loved to throw down when it came to food. His gaze swept over her thick figure and appreciated every inch of her. He felt a stirring in his jeans that he had to fight. Now was not the time to think of the other night. They were in a crowded public place.

"Thank you for bringing me here. I will definitely be back," she said.

A popular song came on through the speakers. Darnell grimaced, recognizing it as a popular line dance. He glanced over at Natoya who was grinning at him. He immediately began shaking his head.

"Don't even think about it," he warned.

She fell into a fit of laughter. She elbowed him and leaned into him. Her eyes grew wide, and she pouted slightly.

"You sure? I can give you private lessons," she teased.

He couldn't help but swoop down and touch his lips to hers in a quick, chaste kiss.

"Not happening," he playfully growled. He

jerked his head toward the small dance floor where people were swaying in unison to the song. "Go on out there. I'll sit here and watch your drink."

"Nah, but I will go to the restroom, though. I'll be back." She sat up and glanced around.

He pointed over to the corner. She grinned, and this time she eased toward him and kissed his mouth.

"Don't go anywhere."

"Oh, I won't, pretty lady," he rasped.

She hopped up from her seat and slid her purse across her body and disappeared into the crowd. Darnell rested his arm along the back of the booth, and satisfaction filled him. It had been a small move on her part, but it was a step in the right direction. He was wearing down the walls she'd built. It would be only a matter of time before they were completely destroyed.

They may have only just met, but deep inside he felt she was the one. She was no Melanie—far from it. Darnell wasn't afraid of putting his heart on the line again. Natoya was a woman who was worth the risk.

10

Natoya stepped out of the stall and walked over to the sink so she could wash her hands. She had to fight the smile that threatened to become a permanent fixture on her face. She glanced into the mirror and almost didn't recognize herself.

She actually looked happy.

Content.

She bit her lip and glanced away before she started grinning like a damn fool. She quickly washed her hands and sidestepped to the paper towel dispenser. A group of women came into the restroom giggling. They were well into their cups. One of them stumbled into the stall Natoya had recently vacated while the other two went over to the sink and began fixing their hair and makeup.

"Will y'all think I'm a ho if I sleep with Jeremy?" the one in the stall asked.

Natoya's eyes widened. She turned away so they couldn't see her face. She was holding back her laugh at the woman's friend's response.

"Girl, I'll kick your ass if you don't sleep with him."

Natoya used that moment to exit the lavatory. She was in good spirits. Those women reminded her of she and Emme when they went out. She missed her bestie and couldn't wait to see her. They would have to come to the Tipsy Cow for sure. Emme would love it here. Darnell hadn't been fibbing when he'd said they had good food and drinks. The music and dance floor were a bonus. She and Emme would be dead center when it came to dancing. They both loved to cut the rug when good music was playing.

Natoya took in the bar and loved the vibe of the place. Everyone was having a great time. She began making her way back over to Darnell. Her heart skipped a beat at the thought of her dark-haired cowboy. She didn't know how he had managed to eat all of that damn triple burger. It was practically the size of Natoya's head. He'd put it away as if it were nothing. She didn't understand how a man could eat something like that and look as good as he did. If she breathed in the scent of the burger, she would gain ten pounds. She reached up and tucked her hair behind her ear. The thought of his hardened muscles and the ridges of his abdomen she had traced with her tongue came to mind.

Lord.

What was she going to do?

Fuck him again, a voice whispered in the back of her mind. Her breath caught in her throat at the thought. Remembering the other day, she was confident she could convince him to stay the night with her.

"Finally," a familiar gruff voice growled.

A firm hand gripped Natoya's wrist and spun her around. She fell forward into a solid form. She glanced up and froze in place. Terror filed her as she met a pair of blue eyes she had hoped she would never see again.

"Cliff," she whispered.

She tried to get away, but he held on to her harder. A dangerous glint passed through his eyes. One that she was extremely intimate with. It was the look he got when he was about to lose it.

"Is that the way you greet me?" Cliff sneered.

How had she thought this man was handsome

before? What had attracted her to him? Was it the blue eyes? The dirty-blond hair that was always kept a little long? His strong jawline? It wasn't until he'd really revealed himself to her that she saw him for who he truly was. He was an egotistical, possessive bastard who had adult-sized tantrums when his favorite possessions were taken away.

Namely her.

"Let me go."

She ignored his smart remark and yanked to withdraw her arm from his hold, but he didn't even budge. She glanced around and didn't want to cause a scene. Cliff lived off the attention. He got off on embarrassing her in public. He wanted to be seen as the all-powerful male compared to a woman who wasn't as strong as him.

"I've come all the way. Haven't you missed me?" He gripped her tighter and wrenched her to him. He had her trapped with his other arm coming around her back.

"Hell no. I left you, remember." The minute the words fell from her lips, she immediately regretted it.

A dark storm rolled along his face. He manhandled her along as he began threading their way through the crowd. She tugged on her arm and finally was able to break free. She wasn't going anywhere with him. How dare he just show up and pull the same damn antics he'd done when they were together.

Well, he was going to learn she was a changed woman.

"I'm not going anywhere with you," she snapped.

He spun around and advanced on her. They were officially making a scene. Dread filled her, but she held her ground. She was stronger than a year ago. This time in Shady Springs had given her plenty of time to reflect on her relationship with Cliff. Their relationship was toxic. There were no other words for it. The constant rotation of women he dragged in, the controlling nature, the assumption that she would always take him back, the lack of respect. She could go on.

She deserved so much more.

She hadn't wanted to share this part of her past with Darnell. She'd had to pick and choose things to share with him when they were talking. A big chunk of her life was dealing with the wrong men, namely Cliff. It wasn't that she was being dishonest or lying to Darnell about her life, but parts of it she didn't want to share with him.

He would probably look at her differently. She'd hate to see pity in his eyes. That was all everyone did when they'd found out Cliff had cheated on her again.

Natoya hoped Darnell didn't see her and Cliff at the moment. She could take care of Cliff and get him gone. She'd left him before and she could get rid of him now. She had the restraining order here in Shady Springs. She would call the police and have it enforced. His family's reach didn't extend down here—or did it?

"Let's go, Natoya. We have shit to talk about." He reached for her again, but a solid form stepped in between Natoya and Cliff.

"She's not going anywhere with you," Darnell growled.

He had a couple of inches and about thirty pounds on Cliff. She stepped to the side and eyed Darnell. She didn't need him to defend her. She could take care of herself. She'd done it for years and didn't need him to step in. Her gaze shifted around, and she saw a few of the guys who had stopped by the table slowly begin making their way to them. She swallowed hard. If she didn't intervene, this was going to go to hell quickly. Cliff had no problems using his fists to get his point across. He'd never put his hands on her.

He'd dished out plenty of verbal abuse her way and may have put a few holes in the walls, but he'd never hit her.

Now, square up with another man, he had no issue in that department. She didn't want Darnell getting hurt on her behalf. She'd seen Cliff in plenty of bar fights and knew what he was capable of.

"I don't know who the fuck you are, but you can get out the way. I saw you and Natoya getting quite cozy over there and I'm here to let you know all that shit ends today." Cliff closed the gap between him and Darnell. He tilted his head back slightly and met Darnell's gaze.

She needed to put a stop to this.

"Who I am with is none of your business, Clifford," she snapped.

He hated the use of his full name. His eyes flicked over to her for a brief moment before settling back on Darnell. There was now a crowd surrounding them. She planted herself in front of Darnell who promptly pushed her back behind him. She grew annoyed and leaned around Darnell's solid figure. What was he doing? This was her battle, not his.

"And how the hell did you know where I was?"

"Your phone," Cliff replied smoothly.

Natoya blinked at his response. Her phone? A shiver went down her spine at the thought that this man had known her every move. There was no reason for him to be tracking her. This whole time she had thought she was free from him, and here he was, he'd known exactly where she lived, where she worked, and even where she shopped. She swallowed hard and made a mental note to do something about this. Even if she had to get a whole new number and phone, she would.

"I'm the one who's telling you that she's not going anywhere with you, fucker. She's with me," Darnell responded.

Natoya blinked at his response. *She's with me?* What did that mean? Was he trying to claim her in front of Cliff and the entire damn bar?

"I advise you to leave now."

"Break this shit up," a big burly man shouted.

He and the other bouncer came barreling through the crowd. Natoya got jostled back as the security elbowed their way between Cliff and Darnell. The one named Rob, who had held the door open for them when they'd arrived, faced Darnell.

"You good, Darnell?" Rob asked.

"This fucker was trying to drag Natoya out of here against her will," he said. He combed his fingers through his hair. He must have left his hat over at their table. His muscles were tense, and his expression was tight. He was pissed off at the very least.

"She's coming with me. I need to talk with her," Cliff shouted.

He tried to shove forward, but the burly security guard pushed him again. Cliff struggled with him, but the guard had to have been a linebacker in his younger days.

"There's nothing you have to say to me. We're done. Leave me alone." Natoya shook her head. She was glad security had arrived. She folded her arms in front of herself. "And don't forget the restraining order, Cliff."

"That piece of paper don't mean shit," Cliff roared.

"All right, buddy. It's time for you to leave." The guard holding Cliff back practically picked him up in a bear hold and began stalking through the bar.

Cliff's shouting was muffled by the music as he got carried away. Darnell turned and reached for her with concern in his eyes.

"Are you all right?" he asked.

She gave a nod and looked away from him. Embarrassment filled her at the thought he'd had to step in for her with Cliff. He shouldn't have had to. Hell, Cliff shouldn't even be here. He must have been bored with his current conquests and figured he could come and get her to go back with him.

"Ma'am, do you want us to call the police? That man is violating a retraining order?" Rob asked.

"It doesn't matter. The police never do anything." She stared down at the floor and felt slightly hopeless. It was a shame. How was a piece of paper supposed to protect anyone? Did she wave it in front of Cliff and it created a magical force field that kept him away from her? She snorted at the thought.

"Are you going to be safe going home?" Rob asked.

"I'm taking her. She'll be fine. We're leaving now. Thanks, man." Darnell slapped Rob on the shoulder. He reached for her and took her hand. "Come on, pretty lady. Let's get you home."

He guided her through the dispersing crowd. Apparently, since there was no brawl, they weren't interested any longer. They arrived at their table. Darnell grabbed his hat from the booth and placed it on his head. He pulled his wallet out and tossed some bills on the table. She didn't say a word. She didn't even know what to say. The little buzz she'd had from her two drinks was long gone.

He took her hand again and led her out of the bar. He kept her close to him as if Cliff would appear and snatch her away. Once outside, she breathed in the fresh air. The night sky was beautiful with tiny twinkling stars and a few clouds that spanned the darkness.

Darnell's friends were posted up outside, leaning against the building. He gave them a nod and headed toward his truck. She scanned the parking lot and didn't see any signs of Cliff. It was then she realized that Darnell's friends were out there checking for Cliff. She glanced back at them, and they hadn't moved. She looked back at Darnell, and the muscle in his jaw ticked. He was still bothered by the situation. They paused at the passenger door of his truck. He pushed her gently up against it and tipped his hat back. He studied her for a moment then reached out and cupped her cheek.

"Are you all right?" he asked in a low voice.

"Yeah." She blinked a few times to clear the itchy feeling of her eyes. She didn't think she had any tears left in them when it came to her relationship with Cliff. She had shed plenty of them during their time together and when she'd finally left. She glanced down at the ground and sighed. "Well, that was Cliff if you hadn't figured out. He's the reason I moved to Shady Springs."

"Yeah, I sort of got that," he murmured.

He tilted her chin upward to force her to look at him. There was no pity in his brown pools, only concern. She inhaled sharply at the gentleness of Darnell. This man had been ready to fight Cliff for her, but deep down, she wished he hadn't stepped in. She needed to show Cliff that she wasn't afraid of him. That he didn't own her or rule her. She was a grown woman, and she didn't need another man to stand in to fight her battles for her.

Otherwise, she was back where she'd started with another man trying to control her.

"If he's a problem for you—"

"You don't need to worry about it," she replied automatically.

Darnell didn't need to involve himself in her issues with Cliff. Yes, they'd slept together once and were out on a date, but that didn't mean he had to go out and fight for her.

"What?" Darnell blinked. "He was literally dragging you against your will, and you're saying I shouldn't have stepped in?"

"I can handle Cliff. I've been doing it for years."

His jaw tightened, and his eyes narrowed on her. She didn't want to appear ungrateful for what he had been willing to do.

She softened her words and sighed. "Listen, I don't want you to get caught up in this mess with him. I wouldn't want you to get hurt."

"I can take care of myself, and let me tell you something," he rasped.

He closed the small gap between them. Her back hit the truck. She was forced to tilt her head back to look at him. Her heart raced while her core clenched from being in such close proximity to Darnell's body. "If any woman was getting dragged out by a crazy ex, I'd step in. My friends would have, too. We take care of people down here in Shady Springs, darling."

He moved her to the side and opened the door. Natoya didn't think he knew anything else but being a gentleman. He assisted her into the truck and then ensured her seat belt was secured before he slammed the door shut. She watched him walk around the front of the vehicle to his side. He turned and faced the men standing near the bar. He gave them a little salute then opened his door. She didn't know what it meant, but she was ready to go home.

The ride to her house was done in silence except for the soft music streaming from the speakers. With the windows down, fresh air filtered through the cab. Natoya focused on the scenery as it passed. She didn't know what else to say. She had a lot on her mind now, and where this put her and Darnell, she was unsure.

Darnell pulled into her driveway and killed the engine. She rested her hands on her purse that sat in her lap, and a small flutter flickered in her stomach. She was going to have to pause this thing between her and Darnell. He exited the vehicle and came around to her side and opened her door. She slid out of the truck and drew the strap of her purse onto her shoulder. They walked in silence to her front door. She took her keys out and turned to face Darnell.

"Thanks for tonight," she said.

Darnell stood near her, and it took everything she had to stick to her guns. Maybe now was not the best time to enter into a relationship with anyone. If Cliff was just going to show up and demand her back, it was going to lead to problems. She refused to allow that man to run her out of another town.

She had just purchased her home and was putting down roots here in Shady Springs. She was not running away from him again. The state of Colorado was big enough for the two of them.

"This thing between me and you," she said. "Maybe we shouldn't. You know? I have baggage and stuff to sort out."

Her words probably weren't making sense, but she had to get it off her chest. Darnell reached for her and brought her flush to him. He lowered his head and claimed her mouth with his. She gasped, which allowed him to take advantage and slip his tongue inside her mouth. Natoya's body betrayed her and melted into him.

He deepened the kiss. His lips moved softly against hers. His hold on her was possessive, and her body responded. Now here she was, trying to tell him that they shouldn't be together, but this kiss proved otherwise. She savored the way Darnell was with her. She couldn't remember any man putting her first when it came to anything. Was she crazy for wanting to put a pause on what was between them?

Her breath caught in her throat when he lifted his head. Had it not been for his arms around her, she certainly would have fallen.

"Darnell," she whispered.

He reached up and slid his thumb along her bottom lip. He leaned in again and kissed her lips.

"Go inside, Natoya. I get it. You have shit to work out, but know this. I'm going to be waiting for you."

11

Darnell guided Benji back to the barn. It was late, and he was dead tired. He'd gotten to the ranch earlier than normal. They had relocated one of the larger herds to a different pasture which took a lot of the hands to help. It could be a dangerous job with as many cattle as they had to move. The animals could be unpredictable, and one could not let their guard down during the process. Experience definitely played a big role in ensuring everyone remained injury-free. There had been a couple of close calls, but no one needed medical attention afterward.

When the barn came into view, he didn't know who was more relieved, him or his damn horse. It almost seemed as if Benji got a little more pep in his step the closer they got to the building. Darnell would make sure his horse was well taken care of before he left. Benji had worked hard today and deserved his favorite treats. They entered the barn and came to a halt. Darnell dismounted and escorted Benji to his stall. He quickly took off the saddle and pad and walked them to where he stored them. He grabbed Benji's brush and some carrots for his friend. He slipped most of them in the back pocket of his jeans so Benji wouldn't see them.

"Here you go, boy," Darnell murmured.

He held out one of the carrots. Benji immediately captured it and crunched on it. He wanted to take the time to make sure Benji was cooled down. He ran the brush along Benji's side. His thoughts strayed to the one place they had been going to for the last few days.

Natoya.

And her fucking ex.

Darnell scowled at the thought of how he'd just happened to look over in the direction she had disappeared in when she'd gone to the restroom. His heart had practically stopped at the sight of her being dragged through the bar.

Benji stepped away from him with a snort. Darnell blinked and shook his head.

"My bad, buddy," he said.

He must have been brushing too hard. He reached in his pocket and took out another carrot and offered it to Benji. His friend easily forgave him at the sight of the carrot. It was one of Benji's favorite snacks.

Footsteps on the old hardwood floors of the barn echoed through the air. Darnell glanced over his shoulder and took in the figure limping toward him with an old wide-brimmed hat on.

Parker.

"What's up, boss," Darnell greeted him.

The eldest Brooks brother made his way over to him and Benji.

"Nothing much. You all right?" Parker asked. He stepped over to Benji and gave him a scratch in between the eyes before he turned and focused on Darnell.

"Yeah. Why?" he asked. He gave a few more strokes along Benji then stepped back.

"I heard you had a little issue down at the Tipsy Cow the other day," Parker said. He folded his arms in front of his chest.

Darnell shrugged and handed Benji the last of the carrots. It wasn't surprising that word had reached Parker. The Brooks brothers were no strangers to having "issues" down at the Tipsy

Cow. They'd had their share of bar fights in the past where they'd ended up just writing checks to pay for the damages. Darnell was surprised they were even allowed in the establishment. He'd guess since their checks always cleared, they would be welcomed.

"Just a little something."

"Anything we need to worry about? I heard it involved a woman."

Darnell gave Parker the quick rundown of him taking Natoya out, then the confrontation. He'd been friends with Parker for a long time. They had even gone to high school together. Even though he was Darnell's boss, he did consider all of the Brooks brothers as friends.

"Wait...Natoya? Isn't that Tyler's teacher?" Parker asked.

Darnell grinned as he led Benji into his stall. He gave the horse a pat on the leg then shut the door. He eyed Parker with the stupid grin that appeared whenever he thought of her.

"Yeah. Miss Grant." Darnell chuckled.

"What about Miss Grant?" Tyler's voice appeared. The kid was an exact replica of his father. All the way down to the hat that never left his head. He jogged over to Darnell and Parker.

"Um, nothing. Just telling your father that me

and Miss Grant went out for dinner the other day," Darnell said.

Parker wrapped an arm around Tyler's shoulder and brought him in for a hug.

"Wait, is she your girlfriend now?" Tyler asked. He feigned a fake punch to his father's stomach.

Darnell grinned at the two. They traded air punches toward each other. He felt the slight bit of jealousy. He couldn't wait for the day when he'd have a little Murphy running around. Maybe a tiny version of himself or a girl with Natoya's eyes.

The air was ripped from his lungs at the thought of Natoya being pregnant with his child. He ran a hand along his face.

He was getting older, and at forty, he was starting to get a little worried. He had always known he wanted children and he currently had none. He and Dane had a great childhood, and he wanted that for his kids. He didn't want to be the father who got mistaken as the grandfather when dropping his child off at daycare or when showing up for a game or a performance.

"I wouldn't say that." Darnell scratched his head. When he had dropped her off at home on Monday, he'd told her he'd wait for her.

And he would.

He understood where she was coming from. He'd been cheated on and left and hadn't had a clue anything was going on. He'd been blindsided by Melanie. Apparently, the whole town had known, and it just amazed him that the information of her infidelity hadn't gotten around.

"Oh. She wasn't in school today. She told us yesterday that her friend was coming to visit and she wanted to hang out with her," Tyler said.

Darnell had wondered if her friend, Emme, had made it. Having her friend with her would help her.

If it hadn't been for Dane and some of the guys, he didn't know what he would have done. He had thought he was losing his mind at first when Melanie had left him. Good friends were so damn important. He'd texted Natoya just to check in on her, but she hadn't responded. He wasn't sure what to think, but he figured she just needed space.

He didn't think she wanted to get back with that fucker, Cliff. His jaw tightened again at the memory of the way he'd manhandled her. Seeing her snatch her arm away from the man had Darnell seeing red. He didn't know what had come over him. Even when he'd confronted

Melanie and her lover, he hadn't wanted do harm to the guy.

Cliff? Darnell had wanted to tear him limb from limb for putting his hands on Natoya.

You're saying I shouldn't have stepped in?

He'd held his breath when the words exited his lips. At that moment, he wasn't exactly sure if she'd wanted to go with Cliff. Hell, or even get back with him. Darnell didn't know anything about their relationship other than it didn't appear to have been a good one. He recognized the type of man Cliff was. He was a good-looking guy who believed he was God's gift to women. He was the type of man who buckle bunnies flocked to, and Darnell was absolutely sure Cliff didn't turn them away.

"If there are any issues, don't hesitate to call," Parker said. He gave Darnell a small nod.

Darnell appreciated it. Even the few guys he'd run into at the Tipsy Cow had been willing to step in the other night. That was why he loved his damn town so much.

"Thanks, boss," Darnell said.

Parker rolled his eyes and grumbled something under his breath.

"Mom sent me out here to find you. She said dinner will be ready in ten minutes," Tyler said.

Parker rested his arm along Tyler's shoulder again. He began leading his son out of the barn.

"And when did she say that?" Parker asked.

"I don't know." Tyler shrugged.

Darnell barked a laugh at Tyler's response. He leaned his arms on the stall door and took in Benji munching on the fresh hay that had been placed in his stall.

"Oh, Darnell," Parker called. He and Tyler stood in the doorway of the massive building. "Why don't you invite her tomorrow? You know we're all getting together for dinner. We always have room for a few more."

"I just might do that. Thanks."

Parker and Tyler disappeared around the corner. Darnell pushed off from the door, satisfied that Benji appeared to be fine. He had almost forgotten that the Brooks were cooking out tomorrow. The entire crew was invited to come. The other hands had been talking about it. The Brooks family were honorable men to work for, and they took care of their employees. Jonah Brooks had even come around. He had always been one mean son of a bitch, but ever since he'd had his heart attack and almost died, he was a changed man.

Darnell headed to his truck and was determined to get Natoya to respond to him. She may have ignored his texts, but she couldn't forever. He was as stubborn as a mule and was set on making her his.

THE RINGER ON DARNELL'S CELLPHONE screamed from his bedroom. He released a curse and snagged his towel and threw it around his waist. He tucked it in tight to keep it in place. He rushed out of the bathroom and into his room. He snatched up his phone and saw it was his brother calling.

"Yo," he answered. His skin was still damp from the hot shower he'd taken. He had smelled to the high heavens, and it was imperative that he get the scent of work off him. He combed his fingers through his hair and slicked it back away from his face.

"What's up, old man," Dane's voice came through the phone.

Darnell grinned at the sound of his younger brother's voice.

"Old man, my ass, I can still whip yours," Darnell warned. He placed the call on speaker and dropped the phone down on the bed. He pulled off the towel and began drying his body. He hated to admit that he had hoped it was Natoya calling. He had left his cell in his bedroom so it could charge and hadn't wanted to miss her call.

"You keep telling yourself that." Dane snorted.

Darnell barked a laugh. Dane always thought he could best him at anything—sports, cards, drinking—but he always lost. "You aren't still at work, are you?"

"Nah, I'm at home. What's up?" Darnell walked over to his dresser and tugged on the drawer. He pulled out a pair of boxer briefs and slid them on. He went back over to the bed and picked up his towel. He used it to dry his hair off more.

"You think the Brooks need another hand?" Dane asked.

Darnell snatched his phone up and sat on the bed. He frowned. Why would Dane be asking that? He'd been working over at the Fergusons' ranch on the other side of town for years.

"I'm not sure. What happened? You not over with the Fergusons anymore?"

"Long story short, they let me go." Dane blew out a deep breath.

It was a shock to hear. Dane was just as hard of a worker as Darnell was. They had both always wanted to work the land and loved animals. Darnell had tried to talk Dane into applying for the Blazing Eagle a few years after he'd been there. They were a fair family to work for, but the Fergusons had talked Dane into going with them.

"What reason did they have?"

"Some bullshit excuse. There has been some funny shit going on over there. Tools going missing, feed bags missing, some vandalism—"

"I know they don't think you've done any of that shit," Darnell interjected.

Dane was an honest man and would never steal. Anger filled Darnell's chest at the thought of someone accusing his brother of such a thing.

"They didn't say it in so many ways, but I drew the line when they wanted to search my truck and shit. I've worked for them for years, and you'd think they would trust me. So when Frank made the ultimatum that I either let him search the truck or don't return, I tossed my keys to him and left."

Darnell gave a satisfying nod. He'd talk to Parker about getting Dane over at the Blazing

Eagle. He was sure they would be able to make something work. They were always working late and short. They would appreciate an experienced cowhand joining.

"I'll talk with Parker about it," Darnell said. He pushed off the bed and went back into the connecting bathroom to hang up his towel. He felt like a new man now that he was clean and didn't smell like horses and cow dung. He glanced at his face and could go for a shave. He grimaced and promised to do it in the morning. "I'm sure they can find something for you."

"Thanks, man. I appreciate it. This pissed me off. Why the fuck didn't they look into the new hands they've hired? I've been loyal as all get out with them, and this is the thanks I get? Fuck them."

"Well, don't worry about it. Everything will be fine," Darnell said. He left the master suite and went in search of food. His stomach rumbled, and it was then he remembered that he hadn't had anything to eat since breakfast. He arrived at the kitchen and beelined it to the fridge. "What are you about to get into?"

"Nothing much. I'm about to head over to the house. I called Mom, and she told me to come over and get a plate," Dane replied.

Darnell paused with his hand on the door. He glanced inside and didn't see anything appealing. Did he want to go over to his parents' home? He knew if he showed up, his mother would make sure he was well fed. It would be good to spend time with the parents and Dane.

"What about you? I'm sure you aren't doing shit," Dane said.

Darnell glanced over at the clock on the wall, and he wondered if Natoya had eaten. She had mentioned painting her house with her friend. Were they both were famished by now?

"I might have plans," Darnell murmured. He reached in the fridge and grabbed a bottle of water before shutting it.

"With who?"

"When did you become so damn nosey?" Darnell grumbled playfully. He hadn't shared anything about Natoya with Dane yet. It was too damn soon. Just when he'd thought he'd made a little leeway with her, Cliff had showed up and put Darnell back a few steps.

"Ah, so plans with a woman." Dane ignored his barb.

Darnell rolled his eyes. He blew out a deep breath and headed into his living room. Maybe a game was on. He could order out for pizza or something. Staying in and relaxing on the couch with a good pie, a cold beer, and a game sounded damn good to him.

"Don't worry about it. But if it falls through, I'll text you," Darnell said. He sat on the couch and reached for the remote. He turned on the television and flipped through his favorite sports channels.

"Well, just so you know, Mom made her chocolate cake," Dane said just before hanging up on him.

Darnell groaned and ran a hand through his hair. Their mother's chocolate cake was award-winning. She'd actually won several awards for it at the county fair. He just may put on clothes and drive over to their house just so he could get a piece. It would be worth it.

Instead, Darnell glanced down at his phone and pulled open his text messages. He checked the one he had sent Natoya yesterday. She still had yet to respond. After a few unanswered texts, what did he say now? He'd asked how she was. Sent her a good morning message, and nothing.

So he sent her a simple line.

Are you hungry?

12

"You picked out a great color for this room," Emme announced. She placed her brush into the paint can and came to stand by Natoya.

They stood and assessed their handiwork. They had just finished the first spare bedroom that Natoya was turning into her home office.

The day had been a day of days. Emme had gone into town that morning, and they'd had a ball. From shopping for supplies to grabbing lunch to coming back to Natoya's home to paint, they'd had one hell of a day. She so appreciated her friend being here. They had laughed so much today, and it was just what Natoya needed.

After the scuffle with Cliff at the Tipsy Cow to ignoring Darnell's text messages, she just needed a distraction. So much had been on her mind. With Cliff just showing up, it had rocked her. She had felt safe in Shady Springs up until that point. She had figured out how Cliff had been able to trace her and she'd turned off the location share with him and ensured he was blocked from calling her. Hopefully that would stop him from knowing her every location. He probably already knew where she lived, and that worried her even more.

But he wasn't going to force her to move again.

She was staying in her little home she had purchased.

And as for Darnell, she didn't know what to do. That man did something to her, and in the few days she hadn't seen him or spoken with him, she'd missed him fiercely.

I'm going to be waiting for you.

Those words alone had almost had her pulling him inside her house that night. Where had he come from? He'd even sent a few texts that she hadn't responded to. She'd seen them and studied them for hours. He wasn't overly doing it and was giving her space, which she appreciated. She did have things to work out, and the main one was if she moved forward with him. That day on the ranch was certainly something worth exploring. They had chemistry, and that man knew how to work her body.

"Hey, what are you thinking about so deeply? Or should I say who?" Emme nudged her.

Natoya laughed and blinked. She turned to stare at her friend who was about the same height as she was. They were similar in build, but Emme was a slightly darker shade of brown than Natoya and wore her long, dark hair straightened, but today it was pulled up on top of her head in a bun so they could work.

"I'm thinking you are right. This color will go great with the desk I ordered," Natoya said. She had avoided the conversation of Darnell ever since her friend had got here.

"Whatever, bitch. I know that expression. You are thinking of a man. One who you haven't even spoken about. What's going on?" Emme rested her hands on her hips and glared at Natoya.

Natoya sighed and walked over to the window. It was getting late, and they had been at this for a while. She stared out the window and took in her neighbor in his backyard. Her cozy neighborhood was full of families and retirees. She loved seeing kids in yards playing and people tending to their gardens. It gave her a true sense of community, and Cliff was not going to run her away from here.

"A lot since we spoke," Natoya said.

"I knew it. Let's open that bottle of wine. Come!" Emme snapped her fingers and disappeared out of the room without waiting on Natoya.

She sighed and followed her friend. She turned off the lights before ambling to the kitchen. Emme pulled a large bottle out of the fridge. She'd arrived in town with gifts, a few being huge bottles of wine that she declared they must drink before she left on Monday.

"Where are the glasses?"

"Over there in that cabinet." Natoya pointed. She moved over to the island and took a seat. Her kitchen had already been remodeled before she'd purchased the home. She had bought two stools that went perfectly with the decor. She wouldn't need to do much in this room. She did want to change a few fixtures and figured she'd hire someone to do it. She didn't want to play around with electrical fixtures. That's where she drew the line.

"Okay, now you met a guy who is sexy and has a single brother," Emme said. She handed Natoya her glass which was filled to the brim with Natoya's favorite pinot.

Natoya giggled and took the glass and immediately sipped it down so that it didn't spill out.

"I did," she murmured.

"You went out with said man and had a good time." Emme stood across from her and leaned on the counter. Her glass was just as full, but she had already taken a couple of sips of her wine.

"Yes, I was having a great time with Darnell." Natoya went into details of how Darnel had picked her up and taken her to the Tipsy Cow. Their conversations had flowed and were never dull. She couldn't stop the silly grin from appearing on her face as she spoke of him.

"Well, if everything went great with him, why haven't you said one word about him since I've gotten here?"

Natoya took a gulp of her drink. She placed her glass down and eyed it. "Cliff showed up."

Her gaze flew toward Emme at the sound of her choking on her wine. Emme coughed a few times and hit her chest. She cleared her throat and stared at Natoya with wide eyes.

"He did what?" she screeched.

"I had gone to the restroom, and when I was heading back to Darnell, someone grabbed me. It was Cliff," she replied dryly. She combed her fingers through her hair. She was sure it looked crazy, but at the moment, she didn't care. She was in her home and probably had paint everywhere. Her heart thundered at the memory of the glint in Cliff's eyes.

"What did he want?"

"What do you think? Probably the same ol' shit. That I need to forget everything and come back to him," Natoya muttered.

"He said that?" Emme lifted her glass and took another sip of her wine while watching Natoya.

"Well, he didn't get a chance to. Darnell stepped in," Natoya said.

"And you didn't call me before and tell me any of this?" Emme's mouth was wide open, and her head tilted to the side. She shut her mouth and shook her head. "I thought we were closer than this. You were supposed to call me that night as soon as it happened."

"I didn't because I'm still trying to process it." Natoya shared what went down between Darnell and Cliff. When she was done, she inhaled sharply and looked at her glass.

It was empty.

"Good for Darnell. Someone needs to stand

up to that asshole," Emme muttered. She brought the wine bottle over and filled Natoya's glass back up to the brim and promptly did the same to hers.

"But I didn't need him to. I can handle Cliff." Natoya folded her arms in front of her chest and leaned against the backrest of the stool. She didn't need anyone to come and fight her battles for her. She was a grown woman and had been doing so for a long time now.

"Really? Handle Cliff? And that's why you went back to him eighty million times when he cheated on you?" Emme arched her eyebrow high.

Natoya wasn't offended. Emme had been right by her side all those times. She was never one to bite her tongue and always told Natoya how she really felt.

Emme lifted her glass and tipped it toward Natoya. "I need to meet the man who wasn't afraid to stand up to Cliff. I'm sure he wasn't used to that."

Natoya bit her lip and stared down at her hands. It was nice to see someone stand up to Cliff. He was always used to getting his way.

What was she going to do? Yes, Darnell had stood up to Cliff, but what if he was like him?

Controlling? Possessive? He hadn't showed any of those signs, but something in the back of her mind kept her guard up.

"I told him we may need to pause what's between us," she admitted softly.

"Don't you dare tell me you are thinking of going back to Cliff!" Emme slammed her hand on the counter.

Natoya jumped. She flicked her gaze to Emme who had a look of disbelief on her face.

"What? Hell no. I just don't know if I'm ready to enter into a relationship with someone again. Cliff put me through hell. Darnell is—"

She cut off what she was about to say. She couldn't even believe what was about to come out.

Darnell is everything.

Natoya closed her eyes and reached for her glass. She took a small sip. She didn't want to go too hard on the wine. She needed to keep her wits about her.

"He's what?" Emme's hand came to rest on Natoya.

Natoya opened her eyes and shook her head. She didn't want to indulge in what she had almost said.

"I'm just afraid that I'm blinded by wanting to

find the perfect guy, and what if Darnell is like Cliff? I can't help thinking how I have a horrible track record of picking men who are shitty. What if I'm only seeing what I want to see and missing red flags? We both know I apparently can't see red." Natoya tried to make a little joke, but it fell flat.

Emme smiled softly and moved to Natoya. She wrapped her arms around Natoya and squeezed her tight. Natoya leaned into the hug and returned it.

This was what she missed most about being near her best friend. Emme never judged her and always offered her honest opinion. Natoya's eyes grew scratchy. She sniffed and pulled back.

"Well, that's why I want to meet him. I'll keep it one hundred with you."

"He's texted me a few times this week, but I didn't respond." Natoya reached up and brushed her hair from her face. At that exact moment, she felt the vibration of her phone in her back pocket. She pulled it out and swiped her finger along the screen.

"Why not?"

"Because I needed to think. My thoughts have been everywhere, and I didn't want to be blinded by the sex—"

"What? You slept with him?" Emme almost choked again on her wine.

Natoya froze, and her face warmed.

Dammit.

She'd forgotten she hadn't told her friend she'd had sex with Darnell. She dodged the napkin Emme balled up and tossed her way.

"How you gonna lie to me?"

"I didn't lie. I just held back information." Natoya chuckled. She opened her messages and saw there was a new text from Darnell. She sighed, and a smile came to her lips at his question.

Are you hungry?

"We are going to have to reexamine this friendship between us," Emme scoffed. She folded her arms in front of her and eyed Natoya suspiciously.

Natoya laughed at her. Seriously? One time she didn't share something with her, now they had to reexamine their friendship? Natoya rolled her eyes.

"Don't go rolling your eyes at me, ma'am. I mean it. How you don't tell me you had sex? Was it good—ooohhh, that's why you sounded funny on the phone the other day!"

Natoya stared down at his message, and her stomach issued a growl.

"Whatever," she murmured. The butterflies in her stomach were in overdrive. She stared down at his question along with the other texts he had sent through the week. Cliff would never have asked her something as simple as if she were hungry. There had been plenty of times the selfish bastard had picked up food without her and didn't even think to grab her something. Nor would he have asked about her day or sent her a simple 'good morning.'

She was tired of having to think so damn hard about finding a good man. They were out there, she was so sure of it. But why was she a magnet for assholes? Cliff was the longest running one she'd been in a relationship with, and before him there had been Brad. She winced at the thought of him. They had been together for about six months before she'd broken that off. Apparently, she had been the side chick and had no clue until his wife contacted her. She'd thought he'd been the worst, and then Cliff came into the picture hollering "hold my beer."

"You down here getting your damn back blown out, and I'm in Fort Clinton sweeping out cobwebs," Emme muttered.

Natoya laughed and glanced away from her phone.

"So do you want to meet Darnell or what?" Natoya asked.

Emme jerked her head fiercely in a nod. "After hearing this, I damn sure do," she quipped.

"He just text me asking if I'm hungry." Natoya set her phone down on the counter and eyed Emme. Her stomach rumbled again. The food she had eaten earlier had been burned off. Painting a room was no easy task. Her shoulders and arms were already becoming sore.

"Tell him we most certainly are, and I want hot wings and fries."

Natoya picked up her phone and typed out a response. Butterflies filled her stomach again. She hadn't seen him in a few days and now she was going to be introducing him to her best friend. Her hands shook at the thought. She just prayed that Emme's asshole radar was working tonight. She had to admit that if her friend picked up on red flags with Darnell, she just might give up on finding love and get a cat or three.

"HE MUST BE SPECIAL. LOOK AT YOU." EMME snorted.

"What?" Natoya glanced down at herself. She hadn't done anything special. After she'd texted Darnell that they were in need of food, he'd offered to grab some and would be stopping by. She'd rushed into her room and ensured she didn't resemble a homeless person. She combed her hair, put on a little lip gloss, and changed out of her paint-splashed clothes. "Leggings and a t-shirt. What's wrong with this?"

"Oh, nothing. Nothing at all." Emme grinned.

They had moved into the living room and had thrown on a movie.

Emme was lounging on the couch and motioned to her. "But you cute, though."

"I just didn't want to look crazy," Natoya muttered. She padded over to the loveseat and plopped down. She pulled her feet underneath her and sighed. "Okay, I'm going to be honest with you and myself."

"What's up?" Emme turned and focused on Natoya.

"I really do like him. I know what I've said in the past about avoiding cowboys and stuff, but here we are," she admitted. It felt good to get that off her chest.

"Don't worry. You know I'm going to be honest with you and what I think."

Natoya nodded. She rested back and turned her attention on the movie they'd picked out. Both her and Emme had a love for action movies, and this was one that they both loved. Her heart raced at the thought of seeing Darnell again. That last kiss he'd given her had left her hot and bothered the entire night. Even days later her core clenched with the thought of seeing him again and kissing him. She rubbed her suddenly sweaty palms on her thighs and blew out a nervous breath. She couldn't even remember reacting like this to any other man before.

The roar of an engine in her driveway sounded. Her heart all but leaped into her throat. She turned and peeked out through the curtains and saw his pickup truck in her driveway.

"He's here," she murmured.

"About time. My stomach was about to crawl out and go forging for food on its own." Emme chuckled.

Natoya stood and left the living room and went to the front door. She paused at the door and inhaled sharply. She tried to will her racing heart to slow down. Through the window, she watched him step out of the truck and amble around to the other side and open the passenger door.

She opened the front door and stepped out onto her porch. She hadn't put on any shoes and was barefoot. She brought the door up behind her but didn't shut it all the way. She waited while he pulled a couple of pizza boxes and a large paper bag from the vehicle. He shut the door with his foot and headed toward her. Natoya's heart sped up at the sight of him. He was dressed casually in a dark t-shirt, jeans, and boots. His thick hair looked as if he had combed through it with his fingers. His dark eyes were leveled on her, and she couldn't move.

"Hey," he said. He came up the stairs and stopped in front of her.

She kept her fingers on the door handle behind her. She locked her suddenly shaking knees to keep from falling over. His gaze swept over her, and her core clenched.

"Hey," she responded. She licked her lips and breathed in his scent. She didn't know what cologne he wore, but she liked it. "I got your messages."

"I figured." He carefully placed the bag on the porch next to them and shifted the pizza boxes to one hand then reached for her with the other.

His hand came to the base of her neck and brought her forward. She went to him without a second thought just as his mouth crashed onto hers. Something like a gasp or moan escaped from her. Darnell boldly thrust his tongue inside her mouth. She could taste the slight hint of his minty toothpaste. She surged forward and gripped his shirt in her fist. She poured everything she felt for him into the kiss.

What had she been thinking?

The kiss deepened, and she'd almost forgotten about Emme until her laugh from the living room reached her. Natoya pulled back slowly. Her head was tilted back as she stared into Darnell's eyes. She still clutched his shirt. He was breathing just as hard as she was. He leaned forward and kissed her.

"Hey there, pretty lady," he whispered. His lips brushed hers as he spoke.

Her heart skipped a beat at his little nickname for her. She stepped back and relaxed her hands. She smoothed out his shirt, trying to fix the wrinkles she'd caused. She glanced down at his firm chest and remembered exactly what it looked and felt like when he wasn't clothed. She grew even more nervous.

What if Emme didn't like Darnell?

"Thank you," she said.

His grin grew wide, and he reached down and grabbed the bag's handle. He jerked his head to the door. "Let's go inside so I can feed you two ladies."

Natoya's smiled and spun around. She opened the door and motioned for him to follow her in.

Here goes nothing.

13

"Oh my goodness, that was delicious." Emme groaned. She rubbed her belly and fell back onto the couch.

Darnell grinned at Natoya's friend. From the moment he'd stepped inside the house, he'd known he was under scrutiny. Emme was a fierce momma bear, and it showed. But Darnell was sure he had won over the bestie. It also helped that the girls had wine before he'd gotten there. Emme was loose at the lips and had been spilling some crazy stories from their college days.

"I agree. Let me clear this table." Natoya had settled on the floor near the coffee table where they had spread out the food.

He had actually been shocked that Natoya

had responded to his text. He had expected her to ignore it like she had the other ones. When he'd seen her response, he had ordered enough food for at least ten people, threw on his clothes, and headed out to pick it up.

His mother's cake would have to wait for some other day. He'd needed to see Natoya. When he'd arrived at her home, he hadn't meant to practically devour her, but the way she'd watched him approach her, it had set something off in him. Not being able to see her, touch her, or even hear her voice had rattled him. Dressed in a short t-shirt that revealed her soft belly, leggings that highlighted her thick thighs that had wrapped around his waist, and her pretty little toes on display had sent him over the deep end.

Hell, if he didn't know any better, he'd say he was already halfway in love with her.

The second his lips had touched hers, he had wanted to chuck the damn food and carry her off somewhere so they could be alone.

"This is going straight to my hips," Natoya grumbled. She pushed up off the floor and stood.

Emme stood and waved her to sit. "I'll get it. You are hosting me, and the least I can do is clear the table." She laughed and began piling the plates up.

"Absolutely not. You are my guest," Natoya huffed.

She tried to snag the plates from Emme who expertly dodged her. She piled up more of their trash on top of the pizza box and lifted it. She balanced everything then stuck her tongue out at Natoya.

"Nope. I got it. You have other company to attend to." Emme smiled. She tossed Natoya an exaggerated wink.

Natoya tried to jog around the table to get to her friend who squealed. Darnell grinned at the two. He stood quickly and scooped Natoya up in his arms and held her to him.

"I got her, Emme." He laughed.

"Hey, you are not supposed to be on her side." Natoya giggled.

She tried to get down, but he held her tight. He did allow her feet to go back to the floor. He held her back against his front and immediately regretted it. His cock stiffened and pressed at his jeans. It was as if it sensed Natoya was near.

"Thanks, Darnell. This woman is too damn stubborn." Emme grabbed a few more things off the table and scurried out of the room.

"What are you doing?" Natoya asked softly.

He leaned down and nuzzled her neck with his face. He needed this. He breathed in her scent and kissed her neck.

"What do you mean?" He trailed kisses along her neck.

Her hands rested on his. She settled back against him and arched her neck. He smiled and nipped her gently.

Fuck, he wanted her.

Natoya turned around in his arms, and he was met with her large brown eyes. Her arms came up to rest on him while she entwined her fingers at the base of his neck. He loved having her in his arms. This was where she belonged.

"After what happened the other night, you are still here," she said.

"You think you are the only one with a fucked-up ex?" he asked. He tightened his hold on her. Natoya was going to learn that it would take a little more than a deranged ex to keep him away. He was here because of her and the woman she was. Darnell dropped a kiss on her forehead. "One of these days I'll have to tell you about mine."

"That bad, huh?"

"Yeah and I'm not sure you have the proper

liquor that we would need for me to tell you the story of Darnell and Melanie." He reached up and cupped her cheek with his hand. He loved how she leaned into it. This woman didn't know what she did to him.

"I look forward to it. I mean, I've heard some things, but I would rather hear it from you," she said.

He bit back a curse. The gossipers in town just could not let it rest. Apparently, the fact that Melanie had cheated on him was still hot news, and for it to be with some rich guy made it even worse. The way people expanded on the story and lied about certain aspects of their breakup was what pissed him off the most. He was made out to be the poor ranch hand who couldn't afford to take care of Melanie. That woman had expensive-ass tastes and wanted to be cared for. She didn't want to work but wanted someone to work themselves into the ground to pay for everything she wanted.

He was actually thankful in the end that she'd left him for the other fucker. Darnell actually felt sorry for him and his pockets.

"Yeah, don't listen to gossip," he muttered. He stared into her eyes and couldn't help but steal a quick kiss. He cleared his throat. "So, did I pass the test?"

"What are you talking about?" Natoya giggled and shook her head. She innocently batted her eyes.

He slid his hands down to her round, ample ass. He released a playful growl and nuzzled her neck again. Her giggles floated through the air.

"You know what I mean." He pressed a hot, open-mouthed kiss to her neck.

A slight moan slipped from her, and the sound sent a bolt of desire straight to his damn dick. He couldn't help the way his body was responding to this woman. He needed her, but he'd be willing to wait.

"Okay, you two." Emme breezed back into the living room.

Natoya spun out of his hold and smoothed back her hair as if they had been caught doing something. Emme jumped onto the couch and looked at her watch.

"I didn't realize how late it was," Emme said.

Natoya moved to go sit on the couch with Emme, but Darnell snagged her wrist and brought her back to him. She wasn't going to sit away from him any longer. He settled down on the loveseat and brought her down onto his lap.

He hadn't paid attention to the time. He'd enjoyed himself with these two and hadn't thought twice about it.

"What time is it?" Natoya leaned forward and grabbed her phone from the corner of the couch.

He settled her across him so her legs were on the cushion next to him.

"Wow! It's almost midnight?" Natoya exclaimed.

"Darnell, are you spending the night?" Emme asked.

Darnell bit back a grin at her seemingly innocent question. He easily read through her bullshit. Emerson was a good friend to Natoya. If she was asking him that question then he'd gotten the answer he needed to the one Natoya had avoided answering.

"I don't know." He ran a hand along Natoya's thigh.

He glanced at her face and found her frowning at her phone. She was focused on something she was reading on the screen. He didn't like the way she was looking and sensed her muscles had grown tense.

"What's wrong, pretty lady?"

"Um, nothing. There's just text that I didn't

see. It came through about twenty minutes ago," she said.

"Who is it from?" Emme asked.

"I don't recognize the number, but I'm sure I know who it is," Natoya said.

"Cliff?" Emme asked. She scrambled to the edge of the couch. An expression of concern was embedded on her face. That momma bear in her was coming out. "But I thought you had blocked him?"

"I did. He must be using another number or something." Natoya tucked a strand of her dark hair behind her ear.

He didn't like this one bit. Darnell gritted his teeth. He knew he should have taken matters into his own hands and dealt with Cliff that night. Sometimes it took using one's fists to get a point across. Darnell had been in his fair share of fights and brawls. The warning Rob had given him when he'd entered the bar the other day hadn't gone over his head. Darnell may not have started any of the fights, but he damn sure didn't walk away from one.

"What does the text say?" Darnell asked.

He tried to rein back his anger. Natoya had uprooted her life to get away from this man, and he just could not leave her alone. He didn't need to know much about their relationship to see how it was affecting Natoya. This Cliff guy was the lowest of lows, and Darnell would ensure he didn't come near her or mess with her again.

"That I can't block him forever and I better call him." She turned her phone off and tossed it back onto the couch.

"And what could he possibly have to say to you?" Emme asked. She folded her arms in front of her chest and tilted her head to the side. "He lost his chance to talk to you, much less even look at you, babe."

"I don't want to think about him. I just want to—"

"Call him," Darnell interjected.

He tried to remain relaxed, but it was getting harder. It was apparent the guy didn't get the point. Natoya had not only left him, moved away from her family and friends to stay clear away from him, and then the idiot showed up making demands of her. The only thing Darnell wanted to know was if he'd ever put his hands on her.

"What? No. Absolutely not. I don't want to feed into his sick little games." Natoya shook her head.

She made to get off his lap, but he held her steady.

"You don't have to speak with him. I will," he said flatly. Hell, he wanted to know if the fucker was still in town. They could meet up and have a little chat face-to-face.

"Darnell, no. I don't want you involved at all. If I ignore him, he'll leave me alone." She turned to him with a gentle expression in her eyes. She ran a hand along his cheek. "I'm certain of this. Please. Just leave it be. Another woman will catch his eye soon, and he'll forget all about me."

Darnell didn't like the response. He wanted to be certain that Cliff left her alone. He tightened his hold on her and pushed down the anger that was brewing. She must have seen the hesitation in his eyes.

"Please. For me? Leave it be?" she whispered.

Her eyes were practically begging him to leave it alone. But that wasn't his nature. He hated having to repeat himself, but it would seem Cliff may need to be taught a lesson.

He found himself jerking his head in a nod. For tonight, he would leave it be. But if the fucker contacted her again, or showed up, he wasn't going to hold back. Natoya deserved to live her life free from being stalked or harassed.

"So, Darnell. You spending the night?" Emme asked again.

Darnell's eyes connected with Natoya's. His mind was made up, but only if Natoya was okay with it.

"Want me to stay?" He arched an eyebrow at her.

She bit her lip and nodded.

He dropped a kiss on her shoulder and tossed a smile at Emme. "Guess I'm staying."

DARNELL BLEW OUT A DEEP BREATH AND SLID into Natoya's king-sized bed. Why a single woman would need a bed this large he never understood. It was actually quite comfortable, and they'd tossed the extra pillows over to the chair in the corner. He didn't even ask why she had pillows on the bed that she didn't sleep on. Her room was simple, and in speaking with her and Emme, she had plans to paint and do a few things in here.

Before they'd ensured the house was locked up tight, Darnell had run out to his truck and snagged his duffle bag that he'd kept packed for the days he stayed on the ranch. The crisp sheets felt damn good on his skin. He decided to stay decent and leave on his underwear.

Natoya was still in the bathroom and had yet to come back in the room. He rested back and stared at the ceiling. He had thought of plenty of scenarios of when they would spend their first night together, but never did it cross his mind that it would be when her friend was in the house. Emme was a good person, and he saw how much the two loved each other.

The door to the room opened, and Natoya came in and shut it behind her. She was dressed in a dark silky nightgown that bared her arms and came to her knees. Darnell's mouth went dry as he watched her walk toward the bed. She had a scarf tied around her head to hide her hair. She smiled and slid into the bed.

"Why are you so far away?" he growled playfully. He tugged on her and brought her flush against him. It felt damn good to have her back in his arms.

She giggled and snuggled even closer to him.

"You didn't even give me a chance to get all the way in," she sputtered with laughter.

He reached out and cupped her face with his hand. They were lying on their sides facing each other. This felt right. To have her with him, in his arms about to go to sleep, this was what he was missing in life.

He wanted Natoya with him at all times.

"Well, now you are where you are supposed to be," he murmured.

"Is that so?"

His cock twitched from their nearness. Natoya must have felt it because her eyes widened, and she glanced down. Thankfully, the covers were over them and she wouldn't be able to see how hard he was for her. He grinned and glanced upward for a moment to try to will his damn dick to behave itself. They weren't going to do anything tonight. Darnell was okay with that. He just wanted to hold her in his arms, and he would be satisfied with that.

"Oh, yeah, pretty lady. This is where you belong."

She pressed closer to him, and his damn cock rested along her stomach. He bit back a growl thinking of how easy it would be to roll her over. He could be inside her within seconds.

Unable to resist, he lowered his head and captured her lips with his. He had been thinking of this ever since the last one. She welcomed his kiss with a sigh. Her lips parted and allowed his tongue to slip inside. Her fingers slid along the nape of his neck and dove into his hair. He loved when she threaded her fingers through his thick strands.

Her lips were soft and warm against his. He tilted his head and deepened the kiss. Her moans fueled something deep within him. He loved the sounds she made when they had made love. That day had been on repeat in his head ever since. He wanted to hear them again, but now would not be the right time. Not with her friend in a room down the hall. His little sex kitten had been very vocal the other day, and he wanted a repeat of that. He wanted to hear her scream his name for all to hear.

And there *would* be another day soon where he'd get to hear her screams and moans. That was one promise he made to himself.

He slipped his hand underneath the blanket and trailed it along her supple thigh. Her silky gown moved as his hand went higher. He soon discovered she didn't have any panties on. His cock hardened at the mere thought that her waiting, hot sheath was close by. He was sure if he checked, she'd be dripping wet for him. It wouldn't take much for his hand to glide over the few inches to where her core was hidden.

He nipped at her lips and soothed them with

his tongue. He lifted his head and gazed down at her. Natoya's eyes were closed at first but then opened. Lust and need filled her eyes, and it took every ounce of strength he had to not shuck off his shorts and slide deep within her.

"We can't," he whispered. His gaze dropped down to her plump swollen lips, and he resisted the urge to take them again. If he did, he wasn't sure he would be able to control himself. He honestly hadn't stayed so he could have sex with Natoya. No, he had stayed because he wanted to be near her. He hadn't liked the thought of her ex making threats through a phone, and it would be just the two women in the house alone. He felt better staying with them.

"I know, but that doesn't mean I don't want to." This woman was trying to ruin him.

Here he was, trying to be a gentleman and not take advantage of her, then she said some shit like this. Her wide brown eyes were pools that he could get lost in. He swooped in and dropped a hard kiss to her lips.

"Don't say that." He groaned.

He wrapped her up in his arms and kissed the top of her head. Her muffled giggle made his cock twitch again. He pulled the covers and arranged them around them so they could be comfortable. She shifted to rest her head in the crook of his arm. He could already feel sleep creeping up on him. It had been a long day, and now that he was lying down, the exhaustion he had felt earlier was returning. It felt damn good to have her next to him in bed.

"Now go to sleep," he said.

"How am I supposed to with this thing between us?"

❧ 14 ❧

Natoya buried her face into her pillow and didn't want to wake up, but unfortunately, her bladder was demanding that she go relieve it. She opened her eyes and cursed all of the wine she'd drunk last night. She honestly didn't want to move. Darnell's firm wall of a body was behind her. His snores filled the air. She couldn't help but admit how right this all felt. She couldn't even remember the last time she had felt so warm, so secure...so safe as she slept.

Darnell's body molded along hers as if they were two puzzle pieces that fit together. Her bladder gave another warning, and she knew that if she didn't get up and go pee, she'd have some explaining to do. She rubbed her eyes and pushed the covers off her. Darnell's arm tightened around her waist.

"Where you going?" his sleep-filed voice rumbled behind her.

She bit her lip to keep from groaning. The warmth of his breath slid along her bare shoulders.

"I have to pee," she whispered.

He kissed her shoulder then released her. She was in awe of the affection he showed her. This was something she certainly wasn't used to. She scurried out of the bed and padded over to the door. She quietly exited the room and went into the bathroom that was located in the hall next to her bedroom. The nightlight in the bathroom allowed her to see a little bit. The house was silent and peaceful. She was sure Emme was knocked out. That woman had finished off the rest of the wine and had cracked open the second bottle. Natoya grinned and closed the door. Her friend was not playing when she said they would be finishing the bottles she'd brought before she went back to Fort Clinton.

Natoya hurried and finished her business. She washed her hands and dried them. She reached up and ensured her silk scarf was still in place on her head before she left the bathroom. She paused outside her bedroom door and listened.

Nothing.

She had to admit that something about the text message Cliff had sent spooked her. She was honestly glad that Darnell had stayed the night. She went back into her bedroom and shut the door. The room was pitch-dark, just how she liked it when she slept. At least this weekend she had people staying with her, but what was she to do when they both went back home?

She'd have to get a dog or something.

She had put on a good front for Darnell when she'd asked him to leave the situation with Cliff alone. Something in his eyes led her to believe that he didn't want to, but he would because she had asked him to. She even hated to admit that Emme was right. Cliff had never really listened to her. Maybe it would take someone like Darnell to get him to leave her alone.

But she didn't want Darnell to get hurt on her behalf.

She arrived at the bed and paused. She bit her lip and thought of Darnell's massive cock that had been erect when they had first got in the bed. She didn't know how he had gone to sleep with that thing like that. She had felt it right before she'd got out of bed to go to the bathroom. The man was certainly blessed in that area, and he certainly knew how to use it.

She lifted the edge of her nightgown and pulled it over her head. She tossed it to the floor and slipped back into the bed. A shiver rippled its way down her spine. Darnell's body was like a furnace. He was asleep on his back with his arm stretched out. She snuggled next to him and rested her head on his arm. He automatically planted his lips on her forehead. Her heart skipped a beat at the move. She wished she could see his face, but in the dark, she barely saw his silhouette.

Her hand came to rest on his chest, and she breathed in his scent. The slight hint of soap greeted her, a suggestion of musk, and something else she couldn't pinpoint, but she knew she wanted to commit this scent to memory as Darnell. She slid her hand down his chest and stopped on the ridges of his abdomen. She paused and waited to see if Darnell was truly awake. She was feeling frisky and needed this man.

She was woman enough to admit when she needed something, and right now, that big cock was something she needed inside her. She held her breath and didn't feel Darnell move. Her fingers grazed the edge of his underwear. She had to admit she was slightly disappointed that he had slept in them. She had hoped he would have come to bed naked, but the man declared that they couldn't have sex then fell promptly asleep.

She closed her eyes for a moment. He must have been tired. She knew he had worked yesterday and that he kept ranchers' hours. He probably got to work around five in the morning. Didn't get off until late afternoon after doing backbreaking labor, went home, picked up food for her and her friend, then hung out late.

The man was probably exhausted.

It wouldn't be selfish if she were to reward him for all of his hard work. Or would it? She ghosted her hand down to his cock and felt the hard bulge. This man was apparently always hard. She prayed these boxer briefs had the little slit in them. She held back her grin when she felt the opening. She reached in and brought his long, thick length out. It almost didn't fit through, but when she got it out she was surprised that he hadn't woken up. She paused before pushing off the bed and slipping underneath the covers. She held back her giggle as she arrived at eye level with his cock. She positioned herself between his legs and wrapped her fingers around his thick member.

It had been a while since she'd sucked a dick, but she was sure it was like riding a bike.

You just got to put one in your mouth and it will all come back to you.

She didn't know if that was a saying, but it seem to fit the situation. She ran her hand along his length and bit back a groan. The damn thing could be used as a weapon. A slight drop of moisture appeared on the tip. She leaned forward and licked it. She bit back a moan at the salty taste. She trailed her tongue over the blunt tip before she sucked it inside her mouth. She glided her hand down to the base and suckled the tip.

Her pussy clenched with need. She wanted to feel him inside her, stretching her as he had before. Her mouth widened as she took more of him. There was no way she could swallow the full length of him, but she was going to damn well try her best. His quick intake of breath greeted her.

"Natoya," he gasped. His voice was heavy with sleep.

The blankets were tossed off her, allowing the cool air of the room to sweep over her. She froze in place with his cock lodged in her mouth.

"Hmmm?" she asked. She refused to move

him from where he was. She giggled and bobbed her head up and down, stroking him with her hands. Her saliva slipped from her mouth and down his length, coating him and making it easier for her hands to smooth over him.

"What are you doing?" he rasped.

She paused her actions and popped him free from her mouth but held him steady with her hand.

"Am I that bad at it that you have to ask?" she teased.

Natoya grinned and drifted her hand up the length of him again. His body trembled underneath her touch. She loved this power she had over him. HIs breathing was ragged, and his cock pulsed underneath her fingertips.

"Fuck no. Don't stop," he gasped.

She licked the tip which elicited a groan from him. She pushed him back inside her mouth and continued working him with her tongue and hand. His hips thrust forward, sending him to hit the back of her throat. She swallowed to keep herself from gagging. The sounds of his low moans drove her crazy. She tightened her hold on him and released him from her mouth. She brushed her tongue up his shaft before encircling the broad head. Her hand could barely close around him, and the thrill of this massive thing pushing inside her made her slick with need.

She moaned when she slipped him between her lips. He thrust harder, and she accepted his movements. His hand came to rest on the back of her head. She gasped and felt her wetness trickle out of her even more.

"You've got to stop," he rasped.

He reached down and yanked her upward. She was not a light woman, but the way this man handled her like she was a doll left her breathless. She landed on top of him, and within seconds his mouth crashed onto hers. His powerful frame underneath hers felt so damn good. She returned the kiss with the same fervor. His big hands held her in place as he plundered her mouth with his tongue.

She shivered at his callused hands roaming down her back and arriving at her ass. He gripped it tight and held her in place. He tore his mouth from hers and trailed hot kisses along her jawline and down her neck. Natoya's breaths were coming in pants. She ached in ways that only Darnell could solve. His mouth found her breast. He suckled, licked, and nipped it before he concentrated on the other one.

Natoya threaded her fingers in his hair and held him in place while he feasted on her.

"Darnell," she whispered.

She had to bite her lip to keep from moaning too loud. She didn't want to risk waking up her friend. He tore his mouth from her and flipped them over to where she landed on her back. He pushed up off the bed and stood. Within seconds he was back, and this time, he was completely naked.

He covered her body with his. She spread her legs wide to allow him to settle into the valley of her thighs. She loved the feeling of him on top of her. His hard body contrasted with her soft one. She ran her hands across his broad shoulders. His hard cock brushed her core, and she whimpered. Darnell claimed her mouth again. She arched upward to him when he plundered her mouth. She gave herself over to the kiss. This man was demanding everything from her. She wrapped her arms around his neck and held on.

His hands traveled over her body, making her desperate for him. He lifted his head, breaking the kiss. He reached between them and lined up the broad tip of his cock to her soaked entrance. Her hips thrust forward; she was greedy to feel him penetrate her. He released a curse and coated himself with her slickness.

"You've got to stay quiet, pretty lady. As much as I want to hear you scream, I doubt you want Emme to hear you." He kissed her hard.

She could practically feel him grin against her lips.

"Unless, that is, you don't care if she hears you."

One powerful thrust and he was home.

Natoya's mouth flew open in a silent cry. He buried himself to the hilt. She tightened her arms around him and remained still to allow herself time to acclimate to his wide girth. She inhaled sharply then blew out a shaky breath.

"Fuck, you feel so damn good," he murmured.

He kissed her cheeks then claimed her lips, capturing her moans. He rocked his hips and thrust forward again. His arms were braced on the bed on each side of her head. His thrusts were slow and deep. She held on to him, and he pumped faster.

Tears slipped from her eyes. The feeling of him pushing inside her was almost too much. He was going so damn deep, and it felt so good, she didn't ever want to part from this man. She tore her lips from his and buried her face into the crook of his neck. She clung to him as he continued to pound into her.

She ignored the creaking of the mattress and focused on Darnell. Waves of pleasure coursed through her body. Her muscles clenched around him. His low groan sent a wave a desire through her. Hearing it gave her a sense of pride. Their skin was now slick with sweat.

"Oh God. Darnell," she whispered.

Pleasure rippled through her. He reached between them. The flat pad of his thumb connected with her clit. She moaned and threw her head back, and he strummed her sensitive little bud while he continued to thrust his cock inside her.

Natoya dug her nails deep into his back. "Don't stop. Keep going. Just like that."

His strokes became harder and faster. The tension inside her was building. Her climax was rushing toward her. She threw her head back and completely let go. Her muscles tensed, the waves of her orgasm crashing into her. A silent scream erupted from her.

"That's it. Fuck, squeeze my cock with your pussy," he growled.

Her body shook from the sensations coursing through her. Her muscles clamped down on him just as he'd requested. He grunted and growled low in his throat.

"Just like that, baby. Fuck, you feel so good."

His thrusts became frantic, almost desperate. His cock swelled even more, and he crested. His hips continued to piston; he filled her with his release. Natoya welcomed all of what he gave her.

He fell forward but caught himself on his elbows to keep from crushing her. She kept her arms around him, not wanting him to withdraw from her. She loved the feeling of him inside her.

He buried his face in the crook of her neck. She kissed his shoulders and ran her hands over his back. This was a moment she never wanted to end. They lay together, unmoving. Their breathing finally slowed to a steady rhythm. Natoya ran her fingers through his hair, loving the feeling of his silky strands.

Emme had given her approval of Darnell. When he had stepped out of the living room and went to the restroom, Emme had given her a wink.

"He's a good one, Natoya. He really likes you."

"I like him, too. I just feel like everything with him is too good to be true," Natoya said. She glanced toward the hallway he had disappeared down. *"He's almost perfect, and it scares me."*

"*Because maybe you aren't used to a real man treating you the way you deserve. Did you ever think of that?*" *Emme asked quietly.*

"*Not really. I try to not compare him to Cliff, but sometimes it's automatic,*" *Natoya said.*

"*How can you get over the past if you won't let it go? Don't compare him to Cliff. He really seems like a genuine nice guy. Just take him for what he's showing you and move forward with your life. You deserve all the happiness in the world.*"

Of course she deserved the best in life. She had always been loyal to the men in her life, even though they didn't even know how to spell the damn word.

"*When did you become so damn wise?*" *Natoya chuckled. She reached for her glass and took a sip. Darnell had brought enough food to feed a small army. He'd put away an entire pizza by himself.*

"*I've always been smart as hell. You just chose to ignore it. Now enjoy this man, girl, and lock him down before someone else does.*"

Natoya blinked and sighed. Darnell lifted and withdrew from her. He rolled them over and brought her into his arms. She snuggled into his hold and knew deep inside she didn't want to be anywhere else.

"What are you thinking about?" Darnell's

voice rumbled underneath her ear. He tilted her chin upward.

Morning was upon them, and the faint rays of daylight were coming through the curtains. She smiled and shook her head.

"Nothing. I was wondering how'd you liked your morning wakeup call." She grinned.

He chuckled and tapped her nose with his finger. "I loved it. You can wake me up like that any time you like," he murmured.

"Is that so?"

"Yeah, and I'll be sure to return the favor, too."

He lowered his head and took her lips in a slow kiss that was so damn tender it brought tears to her eyes. Emme was right. She needed to take him for what he was worth, and this man was worth his weight in gold.

15

"So Darnell here decides that he would be able to mount this new horse." Rashad laughed. He couldn't even get the words out without cracking up.

Darnell rolled his eyes. Rashad loved telling this damn story to anyone who was willing to listen.

Natoya and Emme had agreed to come out to the ranch for the Brooks dinner. This was something they had started doing about a year ago where they invited all of the hands and their families out to the ranch for a dinner. The Brooks family provided everything. Food, booze, and even some music. Some of the hands' kids ran around out in the field near them.

They had a few grills going, and there was

plenty of food. They had set up a wide tent to shield them from the sun's rays. It was a perfect day for cooking out. Darnell picked up his long-neck beer and took a swig. The picnic tables were full with everyone who had shown up for the dinner. Even old man Brooks was there. Jonah was ambling around with his cane, stopping by each table making small talk.

"Now tell the story right. Don't be embell-ishing it as you always do," Darnell said.

Natoya sat next to him, grinning from ear to ear. She and Emme were having fun. The last time he'd seen Emme, she had walked off with Joy, chatting. Natoya and Emme had hit it off well with the girls. Joy, Nykee, and Nasia hadn't batted an eye when he'd shown up with Natoya and introduced her around. She and Maddy had already known each other.

"Embellish? I just tell the story like it happens, and this is how it went. So Darnell wasn't listening to me when I said I didn't think the horse was ready for riding," Rashad said. He looked around the table where Stan, Nasia, and Zach were also listening to him tell his story. "The second he got on, I see him go flying over the horse's head and land right in the biggest pile of shit I've ever seen."

Darnell grimaced at the memory. That horse had been one ornery son of a bitch. He'd been working with him for weeks and just knew the animal would at least allow him to get in the saddle. He didn't even think his ass had graced the leather of the saddle before he'd gotten thrown.

"Oh my! Were you hurt?" Natoya asked. She turned her wide eyes toward him.

He could see she was fighting back the laughter. He wrapped an arm around her shoulder and dropped a kiss to her forehead.

"Only my pride," he muttered.

Laugher went around the table. He grinned and released her. At least Rashad didn't throw in more dramatics like he normally did.

"My back was hurting for a while, but I recovered."

"Is the horse still here?" Nasia asked. She wiped away a few tears that had escaped her. She hadn't stopped laughing since Rashad had started the story.

"Actually, no. It had got loose from the barn one day and ran wild. By the time we caught him, he was miles way and had broken his leg. We ended up having to put him down," Darnell said.

It had been a sad day. Darnell hated to see any

animal injured. But the break had been a difficult one, and then it had gotten infected. Dr. Hutson had tried to save the leg and the horse, but the infection had spread, and the most humane thing to do was to put him down.

"Damn shame," Zach said.

Darnell was surprised the new hand had come to the cookout. He pretty much stayed to himself. Eyeing Rashad, Darnell wondered if he'd had a say in getting Zach to come out today. Darnell knew a few things about Zach, but not much. He was a good guy from what he could tell.

"Hey, you want to go check in on Benji with me?" Darnell leaned over and whispered in Natoya's ear.

She grinned wide and nodded. He took her hand and stood from the table. Rashad moved on to another crazy story of his that had the table laughing.

"Your friends are interesting," Natoya murmured.

Darnell barked a laugh at her comment. He entwined their fingers and pulled her close to him. They walked away from the tent and headed to the barn. It was a beautiful day for a country barbecue. Darnell was happy that Natoya and Emme had come with him. Hell, he was happy to spend so much time with her after not hearing or seeing her for days.

After their morning escapades in the bed, they'd fallen back asleep. It was one of the best mornings Darnell could even remember. Being woken up with Natoya sucking his cock had been a well-welcomed shock. The woman had been trying to take his soul, and he was willing to give it to her.

Once they had woken up, Emme had made breakfast for them. He'd joined them in helping work on small projects around the house. Natoya had wanted light fixtures changed in her kitchen. He'd scoffed at her notion to hire an electrician to do it. She'd had everything he needed, and with the tools he kept out in his truck, he'd had them all changed out for her in no time.

They walked along in a comfortable silence. They made it to the corral where some horses were grazing out in the open. Natoya paused by the fence and stood still, watching them.

"It's so beautiful here," she murmured.

She leaned on the fence while she took in the horses. Some of them had lifted their heads with curiosity. Darnell stood next to her, unable to take his eyes off her. She was breathtakingly beautiful. Her hair was styled in her fluffy fashioned cut. He wasn't sure how to describe it, but it fit her perfectly, showcasing her high cheekbones and her dainty earlobes. She reached up and tucked one side behind her ear. Her smooth light-brown skin practically glowed from the sun's rays. Her pouty lips appeared soft, and he knew from experience that they would be if he took them in a kiss.

"Beautiful," he echoed.

She glanced over at him. Her eyes flicked down to the ground as a smile appeared on her lips.

"I'm talking about the ranch and the open spaces," she murmured.

He took her hand and brought it up to his lips. He kissed her wrist.

"And I'm talking about you," he replied.

"Are you always like this?" She turned to face him.

There was a curious glint in her eyes. She closed the gap between them. She reached up and removed an invisible piece of lint from his plaid shirt.

"Like what?"

"Nice. A gentleman. Caring. Funny. Thoughtful. Affectionate?" she asked.

"You mean am I a human being?" he joked.

He raised an eyebrow at her. He wasn't sure what type of men she was used to—he had a clue, seeing how he'd met Cliff—but what did she really expect? Darnell narrowed his eyes on her. Was she asking if he was just putting on a front? Acting one way but truly an ass? He blew out a deep breath and brought her closer to him.

"What you see is what you get, Natoya."

She bit her lip and studied him for a moment. He wished he could erase the doubts in her mind. He was fighting to get past all of her mistrust issues she had. He wanted to knock those barriers down so she could be free to love him.

Was that what he wanted? Natoya's love? It took him one point three seconds to come to a conclusion.

Yes. He wanted her love and more. He wanted a future with her. He wanted her to bear his last name. Bear his children. Grow old with her.

That was what he wanted.

"I would never lie to you, Natoya," he continued. He needed to make her see that he was a good guy. He was nothing like Cliff. He vowed to prove it to her. "I'm nothing like him."

Her eyes widened. She glanced away and blew out a deep breath.

"I keep telling myself that, but it's hard to get

past my experiences. I want to. My heart wants to, but something in me is telling me to protect myself. I can't get hurt again, Darnell." She shook her head and sniffed.

The walls she had constructed around herself were visible from the moment he'd met her. If he could go back to the other night, he'd punch Cliff in the face for hurting this woman. And if he ever did get the chance, he'd take it without thinking twice about it.

"I get it. Believe me, I do. What I went through with Melanie, it was rough, but I knew that all women weren't like her. I just had to keep searching until I found the right one." He reached up and brushed her cheek with his finger. The wind blew at that exact moment, bringing her hair into her face. He brushed it away and tucked her hair back behind her ear where she'd had it.

"Thank you for being so understanding," she whispered.

He jerked his head in a nod. He took her hand again and led her toward the barn. He needed to check in on Benji and make sure his friend was good and to give him some snacks. They went into the barn, and he went over to where they kept fresh fruit and vegetables for the horse. The barn was long and huge. It housed a ton of horses. Not only were the horses that belonged to the ranch housed here, but some of the hands kept their horses there, and the Brooks family even boarded some for others.

"Come. I'm sure Benji is wondering where his treats are," he said. He handed her two carrots. It was one of Benji's favorites.

"I've always wanted a horse, but my parents wouldn't have been able to afford one when I was a kid," Natoya said. She smiled and looked in on all the stalls as they passed. Some of the horses were nosy and peeked their heads out the doors.

"Same. I didn't get my first one until I started working," Darnell shared.

Just as they arrived at Benji's stall, he stuck his head out. The horse was excited to see them. He greeted them with a neigh then blew out a deep breath. Darnell laughed and rubbed Benji on the head.

"Hey, my friend. See who I brought to visit?"

"Look at you," Natoya cooed. She laughed and hid the carrots behind her back. She rubbed and scratched Benji between the eyes. He loved it and pushed his head forward toward her.

"He loves a good scratch." Darnell chuckled.

"I see. I have something for you," she said.

She brought one of the carrots out for Benji who immediately bit part of it off. She held it steady while he came back for more. She was a natural when it came to being around horses. Some people were shy or scared due to the animal's size. But horses were highly intelligent and could always sense a person's feelings and emotions.

"Such a good boy."

Darnell watched her interaction with Benji. His horse had a soft spot for her. He was gentle-natured and was a softy when it came to the ladies. It didn't matter if it was a human woman or horse, Benji was a ladies' man. He finished his first carrot and turned to Darnell.

"What you staring at me for? She has your treats." Darnell laughed.

Benji butted him with his head then turned back to Natoya who held out the second carrot for him. Benji nickered before biting into the second carrot. He chomped away until the large carrot was gone. Natoya rubbed Benji's neck and had an expression of awe in her eyes as she watched him. Once he was done, he eyed Darnell again who held up his hands.

"That's it. I'm sure you've had plenty to eat.

No getting fat. We have lots of work to do come Monday."

Benji blew out a deep breath again and turned way and went back into his stall. Darnell laughed at his horse's attitude.

"Well, I guess that wasn't the answer he wanted." Natoya chuckled. She swiveled around and leaned back against the wall.

"He'd snack all day if he could," Darnell grumbled.

"Wouldn't we all. Especially if you couldn't gain any weight?" She patted her slightly plump belly.

He growled playfully and came to stand in front of her, trapping her against the wall. He rested a hand near her head and the other on her hip.

"You are perfect just the way you are. Snack all you want," he murmured. He loved the curvy frame of her body. He was never into extremely thin women. He never found them attractive at all. He liked his women with plenty of soft curves. Something he could hold on to. He wanted a woman who he wasn't afraid would break underneath him.

She grinned and tilted her head back.

"See, you saying things like that may get your

rewarded again." She pressed herself forward until there was no room left between them. Her arms slipped upward to where she could entwine her fingers at the base of his neck.

He loved how well they fit together. He was tall, and her being next to him made her appear petite.

"Oh, was that what that was earlier? I was being rewarded for something?" He arched an eyebrow at her. If that was the case, he would keep doing whatever it was that she deemed was worthy of waking him up the way she had. He wrapped arm around her waist to anchor her to him.

"You most certainly were." Her lips curved up into her sexy little smile.

Darnell couldn't resist. He swooped down and covered her lips with his. Those full, plump lips were so damn pliable underneath his. Her moan greeted him. She tasted of sunshine, honey, and a hint of the mesquite barbecue sauce.

This woman was addictive. The intensity of the kiss grew. Darnell poured everything he felt for her into it. He wanted her to know that she was desired. She clung to him as he deepened it. Her hands dove into his hair, eliciting a groan from Darnell. He loved the feeling of her fingers in his hair. She pulled on it, and a ripple of desire flowed through him and went straight to his dick.

But then the yanking on his hair intensified.

He lifted his head and found Benji nipping at him.

"Hey." Darnell laughed. He raised a hand to check to see if his damn horse had ripped any of his hair out.

Natoya fell into a fit of laughter against his chest.

He held her to him and couldn't help but join her. "What are you doing?"

Benji neighed and shook his head.

"I think he thought you were hurting me." Natoya grinned. She moved away from him and cooed and rubbed Benji's head.

Darnell stood in disbelief, staring at his faithful horse. Yeah, Benji had a soft spot for Natoya. He whined and neighed at her as she rubbed him down.

"Okay, that's enough," Darnell growled playfully. He snagged Natoya by the waist and pulled her back to him. Her backside fit perfectly against him. He bit back a groan, her ass connecting with his stiff member. "She's my woman, not yours."

Natoya stiffened in his arms. He bit back a

curse at the slip of his tongue. She looked at him over her shoulder with an eyebrow raised.

"When did we make that decision?" she asked.

He released her, and she took a few steps away from him. Darnell combed his fingers through his hair and walked toward her. He didn't want her to run away from him. They had made great strides this weekend.

"Natoya, I'm not going to lie or sugarcoat anything. I do have feelings for you."

He stopped in front of her. He ached to touch her and have her back in his arms. Her wide eyes held a bit of fear in them that he didn't like seeing. He gently reached up and cupped her cheek. She didn't shy away from him, and that pleased him. She was like a spooked filly. He was going to have to be careful and continue to earn her trust. "I'm not anything like your past and I need you to see that. I care about you. I want you to be happy. I love when you smile, laugh, and enjoy yourself."

Her eyes grew wider. She leaned into his palm, and he brought her closer to him. She trembled slightly, and the urge to protect her blossomed in his chest.

"I do like you, Darnell," she admitted.

"Well, that's good to know." He grinned at her. He would hope she did for her to do what she'd done this morning.

Her body was starting to relax against him. He was going to win her over eventually.

"How about we take it one day at a time. No labels. Just me and you hanging out and doing whatever it is that feels natural between us?" he asked.

She paused and took him in for a brief moment. They were the longest seconds of his life as he waited for her to answer. She finally nodded.

"Okay. I can do that," she said.

He'd take it as a win, and to seal the deal, he kissed her.

16

"I've been gone for two weeks and I've barely gotten a text or a phone call from you," Emme muttered.

Natoya chuckled. She raced around her bedroom, trying to figure out what the hell she was going to wear. She and Darnell had a date.

The past two weeks had been perfect. She had to pinch herself to see if she was dreaming.

"Ouch," she exclaimed. Yes, she was definitely awake.

"What's wrong with you?" Emme asked.

Natoya walked over to her closet again for the tenth time. She stared at the clothes that were hanging in it and moved them around. Again. She finally decided on a cute plaid shirt dress that she'd purchased a few months back. She hadn't worn it yet but figured today might be the day she put it on.

"Nothing," Natoya responded. She pulled the dress out and laid it on her bed. She had the perfect wide belt to go with and she'd find some shoes to throw on with it. She giggled and looked at her spend-the-night bag that was perched on the bed next to her dress.

She and Darnell had been spending a lot of time together, and some nights she slept over at his place, sometimes he stayed over at hers.

"So I'm good to assume everything is going well with Darnell?"

"Yeah, it is," Natoya admitted.

She moved her bag over by the bedroom door and dropped it on the floor. She went back over to the bed and took a seat. She snagged her favorite body butter cream out of her nightstand and began moisturizing her body. It was Friday, she'd gotten off work, and the plan was for her to meet Darnell at his place. He had something planned for her, but he wouldn't tell her what. The man wouldn't even give her a hint at what to wear.

"See, I knew it. Girl, don't let that man go," Emme said.

Natoya glanced over at her phone and sighed.

She just couldn't help but think everything was going too well. Darnell was almost too good to be true.

"What do you all have planned?" Emme asked.

"I'm not sure. He told me to get my butt over to his house, and I guess I'll find out then," Natoya admitted. She grabbed her bra and put it on.

"Oh, a man who plans surprise dates? Girl, confirm the status of his brother, please?" Emme laughed.

"That I can do."

"Well, I didn't want anything. I guess I will go open my bottle of wine, get online, and browse the animals that are up for adoption at the shelter." Emme sighed.

Natoya rolled her eyes at her friend's dramatics. "Well, don't forget you are allergic to cats."

"But what if there is one that is really cute? Maybe I can just take antihistamines for the rest of my life?" Emme giggled.

"Girl, no. You remember what happened when you stayed with your grandmother that week and what her cat did to you?" Natoya chuckled at the memory. Emme literally had welts on her body from just being around the damn cat.

"I'm sure I can build up a tolerance to Benadryl."

"Girl, stick with a damn dog if you are going to adopt. And make sure my fur niece or nephew is extremely cute and cuddly."

Emme wasn't going to adopt an animal anytime soon. This was a threat they both had made hundreds of times because of being single and not being able to find anyone suitable to be with. Natoya did want Emme to be happy. She deserved it. She was intelligent, funny, had a great personality, and a body to die for. How was a woman like her single?

"Tell Darnell I said hello."

Natoya promised she would and ended the call with the promise to phone her soon. She smiled as she finished applying her body butter all over. She stood and went over to her dresser to find a pair of panties. She opened her undie drawer and stared in it.

She bit her lip and had a thought. What if she went over there with no panties on? What truly would be the point? They would just end up somewhere on Darnell's floor. She spun around and decided to go commando. She threw the dress on and finished off her outfit with some cute sandals.

"Who are you?" Natoya stood in front of her floor-length mirror and posed. She barely recognized herself, but she had to admit that she looked damn good

Happy.

Not that she needed a man to make her happy, but she certainly was reaping all of the benefits of having a good man in her life. One who was caring. One who was thoughtful. One who knew how to give her multiple orgasms.

She clamped her legs together to try to beat down the memory of the last time they had been together. Lord, that man knew his way around her body.

She went into her bathroom and fixed up her hair. She wasn't going to put on a lot of makeup. Some mascara and lip gloss would do. Once she was satisfied with her appearance, she left the bathroom, snagged her phone and bag, and walked to the front door. Her phone vibrated just as she was locking up the house.

"Who is this?" she murmured. She turned and jogged down her steps and headed over to her car. She swiped the screen on her phone and froze.

You are going to forgive me.

The text was from an unknown number. Natoya knew who it was without asking. She swiped the message and deleted it. Cliff had been sending her message after message, demanding she call him. And she had deleted them all. When was he going to give up? She didn't want anything to do with him.

She had a new man who knew how to treat her. She put her things in the car and hopped in. She couldn't wait to see Darnell. His place wasn't that far from hers. It was on the other side of town, but it didn't take long for her to drive there.

It was a beautiful fall day, so she rolled down her windows and let the music blast. She sang along with it and couldn't remember feeling so free. She smiled and danced along with the music. One of her favorite songs by Nina Hunt came on, and she cranked the radio even louder. She was a big fan of the R & B singer and had even caught her in concert a few times. By the time the song ended, Natoya was out of breath and felt as if she had performed at one of Nina's concerts.

Another song came on, and she just hummed along with it. It wasn't much longer before she was pulling into Darnell's driveway. She parked her car and cut the engine. He must have been watching for her because he came out of the house at the same time she stepped out of the car.

He ambled down the stairs of his porch, and her breath caught in her throat. How the hell did she get to be so lucky? This man was so damn fine, and he was all hers.

She blinked.

When did he become hers? She hadn't wanted to label anything between them. What they had at the moment was what she needed. Slow and steady. Whatever happened, happened. He was casually dressed in a dark t-shirt and a pair of gray sweatpants. Did that man not know what sweatpants meant for a woman? She bit back a groan and scooted around the car.

"Where's your stuff?" he asked.

Her eyes dropped down to his feet, and she noticed they were bare.

"Well, hello to you, too, and where are your shoes?" she exclaimed.

He walked over to her and snagged her by the waist and brought her flush to him. He dropped one hell of a kiss on her that left her forgetting what she had been saying. He lifted his head and smiled.

"Where's your stuff?" he whispered.

"Um, the backseat," she responded.

If he hadn't been holding her up, she would have fallen to the ground. He grinned and opened the back door and lifted her bag. His eyes widened, and he glanced over at her.

"What the hell is in here?" He chuckled. He shut the door and took her by the hand.

They headed toward the house.

"Oh, just a few things." She shrugged.

If he was dressed in sweats and a t-shirt, she was overdressed. Thankfully, she had other outfits that were a little more casual than what she had on.

"I think I'm overdressed."

"You're fine."

They entered the house, and he slammed the door shut. Natoya found her back against the door with Darnell covering her front. He pressed close to her and took her mouth in a hard, bruising kiss. If she hadn't known any better, she would have sworn he hadn't seen her for days or months.

The man was practically devouring her, and she was not going to complain. His large hand slid along her arms and moved over to her waist while the other held her face in place. She inched closer to him, needing more. Her body was already strung tight thinking of the last time they'd been together. His hand trailed along her hip and underneath her dress.

A moan slipped from her. His tongue stroked hers in a tantalizing dance that promised so much more. His hand paused at her hip. He tore his mouth from hers and stared down at her.

"Where the hell are your panties?" he rasped. His lips burned a hot trail of kisses along her jawline.

Arousal and desire spread through her. Natoya arched her head back to give him access to her neck. Her breaths were coming in pants. He nipped and licked her suddenly sensitive skin. Her core was slick and aching for him. His hand made its way to her center. She spread her legs.

A gasp escaped her as his finger slipped between her folds and connected with her swollen bundle of nerves.

"Jesus," he bit out.

Natoya gripped the edge of his shirt and tugged it upward. She had to get to his bare skin. She sighed at the sight of his chiseled chest and ridged abdomen. Her mouth landed on him, spreading kisses along his firm pectoral muscles. Her hands continued on, and she pushed down his sweats. His hands joined hers and maneuvered his pants down to his ankles. He bent down and hefted her up by the backs of her legs. She wrapped them around him while seeking out his lips.

Their mouths merged together in a deep, passionate kiss that heightened her need for this man. She savored the feel of him, the taste of him. She was addicted to him. His kiss was dominating, powerful, and commanding. She whimpered at the feeling of his hard length brushing her folds.

"Darnell. Please. I need you inside me," she begged. She dug her fingers into his back to encourage him. She opened her eyes and found his dark ones watching her.

He flexed his hips, and his cock slid along her slit. She bit her lip to keep from crying out. If she had to beg this man to fuck her with his cock, she would.

"Is this what you want?" he rasped.

He nipped her chin and soothed it with his tongue. He repeated the motion, eliciting a groan from both of them. She clung to him, digging her nails into his shoulders. He cradled her as if she were the most precious thing on earth. She wasn't even sure how he could hold her up the way he was. She was no small woman. She leaned forward and brushed her lips over his. She rested her lips near his ear.

"Fuck me, Darnell. Let me feel you stretch out this pussy," she whispered. She nipped his earlobe.

A tremor went through him.

"You're going to be the death of me," he muttered.

He reached between them and lined up the broad head of his cock to her dripping entrance. He nudged her opening and sank inside her. Natoya's head flew back against the doorframe as he pulled back slightly then thrust in.

That wonderful, magical feeling of being him filling her up had her wanting to scream. She struggled to breathe. He set a rhythm with his hips. Her cries and whimpers grew with his thrusts becoming more desperate. Natoya's body was on fire.

"Natoya," he rasped.

The sounds of their lovemaking filled the air. The rhythmic slapping of skin, the soft sounds of him sinking into her wetness fueled the desire for her. Her arousal grew with each thrust. She was so close to climaxing. It was just over the horizon, and she was reaching for it. She needed the release that was promised. His cock slipped in and out of her, creating a delicious friction. Her clit was stimulated by the movements. She cried out, unable to hold back.

Darnell stepped backward away from the door and held her up. She wrapped her arms around him, the fear of falling taking over.

"I got you," he growled.

His hips worked faster. His strong hands gripped her ass and controlled their motions. She squeezed her eyes shut and took everything he was giving her. Long, deep strokes that hit just the right spot inside her that sent her flying high into her orgasm.

"Darnell!" she screamed.

Her muscles tensed while tremors racked her body. She buried her face into his neck, and he continued to hammer home. His grunts became hoarse, his hold on her tightened, and his muscles grew taut. He bellowed a yell and tumbled into his own climax.

Warmth flooded her, his release filling her. He stumbled forward where her back was to the door again. The only sounds in the house were their collective pants. She didn't know how long they remained like that. Darnell finally withdrew from her. He lowered her to where her feet touched the floor.

Natoya opened her eyes and tilted her head back so she could look at him. The evidence of their lovemaking escaped her and slid down her inner thighs. Darnell rubbed her bottom lip with his thumb. They didn't say a word, just stared at each other. Natoya felt a stirring in her chest for this man.

She didn't want to believe it could be love. It was too soon for that. Was it lust? Oh, she definitely was lusting after this man.

"How does this dress come off?" he murmured.

She reached up and opened the buttons. It was a simple dress that mimicked a flannel shirt, only it was altered into a dress. She opened it completely and allowed it to drop down to the floor along with her belt. Darnell reached forward and undid the clasp that was nestled in between her breasts. That fell to the floor along with her dress. She kicked her sandals off and stood bare before him.

The heat in his gaze made her feel like the sexiest woman in the world. All her doubts of her imperfections disappeared when this man looked at her. A cry escaped her as he tossed her over his shoulder. He moved so fast she didn't have time to react. He spun around and carried her off to his bedroom.

Natoya grinned. She'd guess that whatever plans he had for them, they weren't going to make it.

17

Darnell entwined his fingers with Natoya as they walked along the fairgrounds. It was the night of the Harvest Festival. It was an annual event that was big for their town. There were carnival rides, games and activities for the kids. There were even small rodeo events to participate in. He and Natoya had enjoyed food from several vendors and tried out a few beers from local breweries.

He had to admit he'd never seen this woman smile so much as she had been lately. He liked to think he had a hand in it. He couldn't be more pleased with the direction of their relationship. They still hadn't labeled each other, but at the moment he didn't mind. He felt that she cared for him. If they weren't together, they were either texting each other or talking on the phone.

Had he caught feelings for this woman? One hundred percent yes. He held back sharing them with her because he didn't want to scare her off. He had promised slow, and he was a patient man, and she was well worth the wait.

"I think the line dance contest is about to start." Natoya grinned and tugged him behind her.

He laughed at her excitement. She had said that Joy, Nykee, and Nasia had entered and she wanted to cheer them on. They arrived at the makeshift dance floor and found a crowd of people surrounding it.

"Why didn't you enter?" he pulled her closer to his side, not wanting an inch between them. He was pleased how she leaned into him and rested her head on his chest.

She tilted her head back and eyed him. "Because that would be cheating! Why would a line dance teacher enter a contest?" She looked at him as if he'd grown another head.

He burst out laughing at her expression.

"You'd have a better chance at winning." He snorted.

"And if I lost, how would that make me look?

That would be bad for business," she said with a straight face. She held it for a brief moment before falling into a fit of laughter.

Darnell dropped a kiss to the top of her head. This woman had a sense of humor that rivaled his. That was why they were so damn good together. It wasn't just about the sex. That was out of this world, but her personality meshed well with his. They loved the same type of movies, food, and horses.

Their attention was captured by the dancers who started filling the dance floor. They had numbers posted on their backs. There was more than he would have imagined entering a line dancing contest.

"Wow. Look at all of the people. Do you see the girls?" Natoya tried to stand on her tiptoes to see.

Darnell scanned the floor and caught sight of Nykee first. Joy and Nasia were standing near her. They were all making sure their numbers were on their backs.

"There they are." He pointed over in the corner where they stood.

"They've come a few times to the class. They'd better place well if not win," Natoya said.

She pulled away and screamed out the girls'

names. They turned around and found her. They all waved and grinned like the fools they were. Darnell smiled at their silliness.

And they had thought they were going to get him to enter with them. Hell no, he wasn't going to be making a laughingstock of himself in front of all of these people.

He turned his head and paused. He couldn't believe his eyes, but then again, he should have known better.

"I'll be damned," he murmured. In the opposite corner he caught sight of a familiar figure who was short and plump with salt-and-pepper hair that was pulled up into a high bun.

His mother.

"What is it?" Natoya asked. She tried to see where he was staring off to.

"My mother is out there." He laughed. He glanced around to see if he could find his father. If his mother was here, then the old man wouldn't be too far.

"Are you serious?" Her eyes grew wide. She looked out at the crowd. "Which one is she?"

He glanced back at his mother, and when she turned around, he saw her number. He rolled his eyes and shook his head. His lips curved up into a smile.

He pointed in the direction and leaned down toward Natoya's ear.

"Only my mother would have sixty-nine as her number." He chuckled.

Natoya giggled and covered her mouth with her hand.

"Aww...she's cute and she can dance? What happened with you?" She nudged him with her elbow.

"Murphy men don't dance," he grumbled. He wrapped his arms around her and pulled her back toward him. He hesitated for a moment before he leaned down near her ear so she could hear him. The announcer had just come on and was speaking into the microphone. "Would you be okay meeting her and my father?"

Natoya stiffened. She glanced over her shoulder at him then nodded. Something passed through her eyes that he couldn't read. Her muscles relaxed a bit.

"Sure. I'd love to meet them."

Darnell straightened to his full height and felt a satisfaction. They were most definitely headed in the right direction.

"THEY ALL WERE CHEATED," NATOYA HUFFED. She folded her arms in front of her chest and scowled.

Neither of the girls nor Darnell's mother had won. Some young girl had and was currently being presented a Harvest Moon Line Dance trophy.

"It'll be all right. They have next year." He chuckled.

Applause went around as the young lady accepted her trophy from the announcer.

"That's true, but I just had high hopes that someone I knew would have won." She grinned. She turned to him and shrugged.

The crowd began to disperse, and he wanted to catch up with his parents before they disappeared. He had finally found where his father was watching the contest.

"Are you still okay with meeting my parents? If you don't want to, it's fine. I just want to run over and say hi," he said. He didn't want to pressure her into meeting them. It was a big step, even though they were out at a festival. He already knew his mother was going to love Natoya. They both enjoyed dancing and had a few other things in common.

"Yeah, I don't mind meeting them. You met

Emme, and she's as close to a sister as I have," she said.

He took her by the hand and navigated through the crowd. He kept his eyes on his father until they were able to get to them. "Mom!"

About three women turned around. He grinned and pointed to the one person who didn't.

"Amelia!" he called out.

This time his mother spun toward him, her face bright and a wide smile spread along her face.

"Look who is here, Tommy." She slapped his father across the stomach.

He and his father were the same height and had the same coloring. Most of his and Dane's features were that of their father. She moved forward but stopped when Natoya came to stand by him. Her eyes grew wide as saucers, and her grin spread even more.

He wasn't sure why, but he was slightly nervous at introducing Natoya to his parents. They both moved forward so a group of people could get by them.

"You did good out there," he said.

"I didn't know you were coming," his mother

said. She motioned to his father. "I had to threaten him to come."

"Don't go telling stories, Amelia. You know I was coming for the beer and food." His father chuckled. He patted his slightly round belly.

Darnell wasn't shocked by his father's admission. There was only one real reason his father would come out of the house on a Saturday night. Food. He did love to eat as much as Darnell did. His father motioned to Natoya. "And who do we have here?"

"Mom and Dad, this is Natoya." Darnell motioned to her. He grinned as he continued. "Natoya, these are my parents, Tommy and Amelia Murphy."

"It's so nice to meet you," Natoya said. She stepped forward and shook both of their hands.

Darnell tried to ignore the way his mother's gaze flickered between him and Natoya. It hadn't mattered that he hadn't said *girlfriend* before Natoya's name, his mother was already going to assume it. He could see the wheels in her brain spinning.

"You are so pretty, my dear," his mother said.

Her eyes twinkled, and Darnell bit back a groan. He hadn't mentioned Natoya to his parents, and his mother was going to give him an earful.

"Where has my son been hiding you?"

He rolled his eyes and shook his head.

"I haven't been hiding her," he muttered. He went over and wrapped his mother up in a hug. He kissed her cheek and whispered, "I'll explain everything later. Promise."

He didn't want to put Natoya on the spot. He would stop by his parents' home and explain later. Their current status of a relationship was too complex to go into with hundreds of people surrounding them.

"You need to come by the house. Dane has been by lately more than you have." She patted him on the cheek.

He got her message loud and clear. He was slacking in the son department. He chuckled and nodded. "Yes, ma'am."

"And bring your friend," his father said. "I'm sure your mother wouldn't mind cooking for everyone."

"That sounds nice," Natoya said.

Darnell's eyebrows rose high at her comment.

She smiled at his father. "I will never turn down a good home-cooked meal."

"My mother is an amazing cook and baker," Darnell shared.

Amelia practically beamed at his compliment. Not that she didn't already know that. She'd been feeding him for forty years and his father even longer.

"Come on, woman. Let the young ones have some fun." His father wrapped an arm around Amelia's shoulder.

She sputtered and tried to speak, but he patted her on her backside. His mom flushed bright red at the move.

"They didn't come to the festival to hang out with old farts like us."

"Oh, you hush your mouth, Tommy Murphy," he mother breathed. She gave a wave as her husband led her away from them.

Darnell owed his father a favor. If he hadn't taken her way, Mom would have stayed here and still tried to grill him and Natoya even though he'd promised to stop by.

"Your parents are cute," Natoya said. She took his hand in hers and leaned into him. "I can definitely see you in your father. Your eyes are the same."

"Thank you for meeting them," he said. It

meant a lot to him that she had been willing to just say hello to them. This just proved that he was wearing down the walls she had built around herself.

They walked along stands of people trying to hawk their wares. Kids running around, music blaring from speakers, the night sky littered with twinkling stars, and the good ol' country air.

"You don't have to thank me for meeting your parents. It would have been rude considering they were not too far from where we were standing," she said. She rested her head against his arm.

"But still. You could have said no."

"But I didn't." She tightened her arm around his.

She was right about that. She didn't say no. Natoya perked up and let out a squeal. She pointed to a stand with a row of ducks and shotguns. There were huge stuffed animals being offered as a prize.

"Please tell me you know how to shoot a gun!"

"What did you just ask me?" He would have been offended if she hadn't had that little twinkle in her eyes.

Her laughter floated through the air. He

allowed her to lead him over to the game. He shook his head and pulled out his wallet. Looked like he was going to have to show his little lady a good time and apparently win her a bear.

❧ 18 ❧

Natoya walked around her classroom and ensured the kids had cleaned up their mess. It had been a long day, and she was both happy and sad to be back at work. Her weekend had been wonderful. Matter of fact, the past month had been amazing. She had got to spend time with Emme, tackle her ongoing list for her house, spend time with Darnell and get to know him.

Natoya felt that silly grin of hers come onto her face at the thought of him. She'd gotten to see him around his friends on the Blazing Eagle Ranch and when they went out. Everyone had such good things to say about him. She didn't know if he had put them up to it, but it would appear they all loved him and wanted to see him happy.

She glanced around the room and didn't see much out of place. She made her way back to her desk so she could do a few things before she left. Today was not going to be one of those days where she would be staying late.

She sat at her desk and typed out a few commands on her computer. She was going to have to start entering mid-term grades. She glanced down at her watch and figured she could do this from home. She just didn't want to stay in the school any longer today. It looked as if they had another beautiful day on their hands, and she wanted to get some sun. Her phone vibrated from where it sat on the corner of her desk. She smiled and grabbed it. Darnell was probably texting her.

He hadn't come by yesterday since he had gotten off work late. He'd had a rough day and was supposed to be back there super early this morning. Last night, she'd called him, and they had talked on the phone until well after midnight. Even when she'd reminded him that he had to get up early for work, he'd brushed her off, ensuring he would be fine.

Her smile slowly died as she looked at the text message. It was from the unknown number.

You haven't called me.

She swallowed hard and set her phone back down on the table. Why couldn't Cliff leave her alone? She hadn't responded to him every single time he'd texted her and she'd hoped he would have just forgotten all about her. She stood and gathered her belongings and tossed them into her bag. She would work on grades at home on her laptop.

She closed up her room and locked the door. She made her way down the hall. For once, she wasn't the last person to leave. There were still plenty of students and staff in the building.

"See you tomorrow, Natoya!" Holly called out from her room.

"Have a good one!" Natoya paused at Holly's room and waved at her. She put on a bright smile and kept going. She was not going to let Cliff ruin her day. She took her phone out of her bag and pulled up the text. She blocked that number as she should have done a long time ago. She had just deleted all of his messages but hadn't even thought about blocking it.

It was done, and she was going to keep her peace. She didn't want to go and get a different phone number. That wouldn't be fair to her. It would be a pain in the butt to have to start over. She'd had this number since college.

She pushed open the door that led outside near the teacher's parking lot. She would go home, change her clothes, and maybe even go for a walk. She glanced at the sky and took in the bright sun, the warm air, and figured it would be a good plan. Maybe she would even stop and grab a bite on her way home so she wouldn't have to try cooking anything. She thought back to the cookout at the ranch and how delicious that food was.

Now she wanted some barbecue.

She racked her brain and figured she could look it up and see where she could get some barbecue from. She knew not to just stop anywhere. She wanted finger food that would get her full and sleepy. She snorted at that.

Maybe she could text Darnell and find out where to go. Or maybe she could tell him she was hungry, what she wanted, and let him take care of it.

Yup, that might be the best idea. Maybe he could come over to her place or she could go over to his. Either way, she could get her food and maybe something extra. She grinned and hurried over to her car. She dragged her bag up on her shoulder and reached for the handle of her driver's door.

"Just going to ignore me, huh?" a voice growled.

She was whipped around and pushed back against her car with a force that snatched her breath away. Fear took over her as she stared up into Cliff's angry gaze.

"What do you want with me?" she breathed. She couldn't move. Her feet felt as if they were glued down onto the concrete.

"You've blocked me, and I don't like that shit one bit," Cliff snarled.

"We are no longer together, Cliff. There is nothing for us to talk about." She looked around and didn't see anyone in the staff lot. She had thought about screaming, but would anyone hear her?

"How long are you going to play this little game?"

"A game? You think I'm playing a game? I'm tired of your crap. You don't care about me. Matter of fact, I don't think you've ever cared about me!" she snapped at him. She had never raised her voice at him. No matter how many times he'd yelled, thrown things, she had just walked away from him. But today, she wasn't going to take his shit. He needed to leave her the hell alone. "I blocked you, moved away from my family and friends to get away from you. What else do I have to do to get it through your thick head? We are done!"

He pushed her back against her car. She hadn't even realized that she had moved toward him.

"Now don't go getting brave now, Toya," he snarled.

She hated having her name shortened. Toya wasn't her name. Her parents had named her Natoya. As many times as she had told him that, it was one of the many things he never listened to her about. Something as simple as her damn name.

"Don't look like your little guard dog is here to save you."

Natoya shivered as his hand crept up toward her throat. His evil grin spread across his face, and it sent a wave of fear through her. Had she pushed him too far?

"Leave me alone, Clifford," she whispered.

"Now why would I do that? You belong to me." He chuckled. He stroked her chin with his thumb and studied her.

His touch made her skin crawl. There used to

be a day where she would have welcomed his caress. Now all it did was make her want to jump into boiling hot water to cleanse herself. She wanted to tear herself away and run far from him.

He narrowed his eyes on her. "Even if you've spread those legs of yours for him, I'll forgive you."

"You'll forgive me?" Her voice ended on a squeak. Was this man deranged? Had he lost the last sense that the good Lord had given him? He was going to forgive her? After all of the women he'd cheated on her with? All the verbal abuse. The lies. He was going to forgive her for moving on from him?

"Yeah. Come back home, baby. It'll be you and me. Just like the old days." Cliff grinned, and it was as if he truly believed this was all he would have to do to get her back. Just like the old days where he'd be caught cheating on her and she would take him back?

She wasn't the same woman she was a year ago, much less three years ago. That woman was long gone. The new Natoya had a backbone, and she wasn't going to put up with his lies and deceit. She deserved so much better. She deserved a man who cared for her. Who looked out for her. Wanted to see her happy. A man who made her body sing.

Darnell's face flashed before her eyes.

A man who was patient and willing to wait until she was ready for him.

"No."

Cliff's smile disappeared. A dark storm rolled across his face. She'd seen this look before. Fear took hold of her. Yeah, she'd pushed him entirely too far. He gripped her by her shirt and pulled her away from her car. She scrambled and tried to get his hands off her.

"What did you say?" he growled.

"I said no. Get off me!" she cried out. Her bag fell to the ground.

She broke free and tried to run, but his strong arm wrapped around her waist and lifted her from the ground. She kicked and screamed. She tried to elbow him, but she missed.

"I'm done playing with you, Toya. You're coming home with me," Cliff snapped.

His arm around her waist was tight, and she couldn't pry herself out of his hold.

"Put me down." She twisted around and threw another elbow.

This one connected with the side of his head. His hat went flying off his head. He stumbled back, and his grip on her loosened. Just as her feet touched the ground, a figure slammed into Cliff, knocking them into a minivan beside them. Natoya fell forward onto her knees. She glanced up and caught sight of Darnell on Cliff.

She inhaled sharply at the sight of Darnell swinging his fist and landing a punch to Cliff's face. She cringed at the loud sound of some bones cracking.

"Miss Grant!" Tyler skidded to a halt by her. His gray eyes were wide with fear. He gripped her hand and helped her up. "Come on. We need to move."

"But Darnell—"

"He told me to get you out of the way. Mrs. Baker heard you scream and called the police," Tyler said.

She turned toward Darnell and Cliff who were trading blows. Clifford got the upper hand on Darnell for a split second before he blocked a blow with his arm and landed two of his own that sent Cliff down to the ground.

Sirens cut through the air and grew closer. Tyler took Natoya by the hand and practically dragged her toward a patch of grass near the school. Police cruisers flew into the parking lot with their lights flashing. Natoya glanced around and took in the few staff who had ventured outside the school. Her vision blurred as tears came forward.

"Are you hurt, Miss Grant?" Tyler asked. He had yet to let go of her hand.

She glanced at him and shook her head.

"No. He didn't hurt me," she said. Her gaze strayed back over to where Darnell stood speaking with a deputy. She needed to go to him to make sure he was all right.

"Who is that man?" Tyler asked. "Was he trying to kidnap you?"

"It's complicated, honey. But what you did was brave. Thank you," she said. She rested her hand on his shoulder.

Tyler stood taller.

"My daddy said that a Brooks always steps in to help when someone is in trouble." Pride rang in his voice.

She smiled through the tears that streamed down her face. She reached up and wiped the wetness from her cheeks. She released Tyler's hand and motioned over to Darnell.

"I need to speak with Darnell," she said.

As if feeling her gaze on him, he turned and searched the lot for her. Their eyes met, and he visibly relaxed.

"I'm coming with you," Tyler said.

"No, you stay here."

"But he was picking me up to take me home since I had to stay after school," Tyler said. He pulled his hat off and scratched his head before returning it in place.

Natoya glanced around and saw Holly standing near the doorway. She caught Holly's eye and motioned to Tyler. Holly gave a nod and waved for him to come to her.

"Go and stay with Mrs. Barker while I speak with Darnell and the deputies," she said.

He went to argue with her, but she held up a hand. He didn't need to be around for the conversation she was sure she would need to have with the cops.

"Please. You did a good job helping me. Now I need to keep you safe."

Tyler nodded then spun on his heels and jogged over to where Holly was standing by the door. Natoya inhaled sharply and began making her way over to Darnell and the deputies. Cliff was on the ground and handcuffed. She arrived near Darnell who immediately spun to her. There was a small cut on his top lip while a bruise was forming on his right jawline. His shirt was ripped down and hung slightly off him. His eyes softened when his gaze landed on her.

"Are you all right?" he asked. He brought her to him and wrapped his arms around her.

Unable to speak, she nodded and leaned her forehead against his chest.

He pulled back and took her in. "He didn't hurt you, did he?"

"No. I'm okay," she whispered.

Her gaze landed on Cliff who was openly staring at her. His scowl was embedded on his face. She didn't even want to know what possessed him to seek her out at her job. Harassing her on the phone and now this? Even this was a bit much for him.

"You're Miss Grant?" a voice near her asked.

She turned and watched a deputy, who appeared to be younger than her, step closer to her and Darnell.

"Yes, I'm Natoya Grant." She cleared her voice.

Darnell kept an arm around her waist and held her near him. She assumed they would want to speak with her. She definitely wanted to share with them that she had an order of protection in place against Cliff.

"I'm Deputy Holmes," the officer announced.

"I'm told that you were involved in an altercation with Mr. Neil before the fight. We're going to need you to ride down to the station with me for your full statement."

"She can do her statement here," Darnell growled.

His muscles tensed, and she got the sense that he wasn't going to let her out of his sight.

"Standard procedures—"

"Seriously? You can't ask her your questions right here?" Darnell interjected again.

Natoya rested a hand on his chest to calm him down. The last thing they needed was for him to be placed in handcuffs, too, but she actually agreed with him. Why did she need to go down to the station? She turned to the deputy.

"You can ask me your questions here," she said. She'd seen enough cop shows that left her a little leery of going into a police station. They would probably try to put the blame on her for Cliff acting crazy on her. "I have nothing to hide."

Deputy Holmes sighed and took out a note-book and pen.

"How do you know Mr. Neil?" Holmes asked.

"He's my ex-boyfriend, and before we get started, can I just say that I have an order of protection against Clifford, and he knows that," she said.

The deputy's eyebrows shot up. He glanced over in the direction of where the other officers were placing Cliff in the back of his squad car.

"That is certainly information we need to know," he murmured. He scribbled something down on his notepad. He glanced back up at her. "Why is there an order of protection?"

"Long story short, Officer, for this exact reason. He has stalked me, harassed me, and just won't leave me alone," she said.

"Do you know why he is here?" The deputy wrote a few more notes down.

"He wanted me to go back to Fort Clinton with him," she said.

Darnell swore beside her. She blew out a deep breath. Her gaze moved over to the car Cliff was in. The officer slammed the door shut and moved to driver's door and got in. Holmes continued asking her questions. Darnell stood by her side. He chimed in only when Holmes directed a question to him. When asked, he shared that he'd heard her scream when he was coming out of the school and saw Cliff attacking her. That's when he ran over and intervened.

"And your relationship to Miss Grant?" Holmes asked Darnell.

He glanced over at her before answering.

"We're seeing each other," Darnell admitted.

Holmes didn't bat an eye at the answer. Natoya was grateful for Darnell being there. She didn't know what would have happened had Cliff got her into his vehicle. She just knew that she would have kept fighting him the entire way. She shuddered to think of what could have happened.

"Will he be under arrest?" she asked.

"If he is violating a court order to stay away from you, then yes. From what we gathered so far, he was trying to abduct you. Would you agree with that?"

Natoya hesitated in answering. Was Cliff trying to abduct her? Hell yeah. He'd had every intention of making her go back with him. She couldn't look over at Darnell. She could feel the anger radiating from him. She was so damn tired of dealing with Cliff that she wasn't going to hide the truth anymore. In the past, she would downplay things he had done to her, but no more. He needed to pay for his actions.

"Yes. I believe he was going to force me to go to Fort Clinton with him."

"Are you going to check in on Miss Grant?" Tyler asked.

Darnell drove up to the home that Tyler shared with his parents on the ranch. He parked in front of the house. Tyler hesitated before getting out of the truck. His little friend appeared to be worried about his teacher.

When he'd arrived at the school, he'd had to go inside to collect Tyler who had stayed afterward for a science club meeting. He had missed the bus, and Maddy had asked him to grab Tyler and bring him home as a favor. He'd wanted to stop by Natoya's room and surprise her, but her room was dark and locked up. He'd figured she'd finally left on time for once.

He and Tyler had just stepped out of the

building when a scream caused him to freeze in his steps. He took in a man standing next to a car but hadn't seen the woman until she'd tried to run away but was lifted off the ground.

Darnell had practically seen red when he'd realized that it was Cliff and Natoya.

Another teacher had come out of the building behind them. What happened next Darnell vaguely remembered. He'd taken off running toward Natoya. The second Cliff dropped her to the ground, Darnell had slammed into him with a shoulder to his gut.

He blinked and turned back to Tyler.

"Yeah. I'm going to go over to her house and make sure she's good."

He and Tyler hadn't left until Natoya was in her car and driving off. The door to the house opened, and Parker came strolling down the stairs. The eldest Brooks brother limped toward them. Tyler opened his door and hopped down from the truck and met his father. Parker threw an arm over his son's shoulders and came to stand by Darnell's vehicle. Tyler was talking a mile a minute, trying to tell Parker what had happened at the school.

"What's up, boss?" Darnell rolled his window down further. He glanced at his knuckles and saw he was going to need to get some ice on them fast. His right hand was swollen and sore. He stretched his fingers out and grimaced.

"Ran into a little trouble, I hear." Parker squeezed Tyler on the shoulder.

"Darnell had me get Miss Grant and take her away so she didn't get hurt," Tyler said.

"That's real honorable of you, son," Parker said. He motioned to the house. "Why don't you go on in the house and check on your mother and sister?"

"But, Dad—"

"Tyler," Parker murmured. He patted Tyler on his head and jerked his head to the house.

Tyler turned back and gave Darnell a wave.

"See you later, Darnell," the kid said.

Darnell bit back a grin at the disappointment on his face. He knew when he was being sent away so grown folks could talk.

"Thanks again, buddy. You helped out a lot," Darnell said, trying to soften the blow.

Tyler smiled and then turned around and took off running to their house. He disappeared inside, and Darnell was sure he was off to tell Maddy what had happened.

Darnell focused on Parker. He blew out a

deep breath. "Look, Parker. I'm sorry Tyler had to see—"

"I'm not worried about him seeing you whoop some jerk's ass. You do know who his father and uncles are, right?" Parker smirked. He rested a hand on the truck and tipped his hat back. "Now who is this guy, and do we need to pay him a visit?"

Darnell chuckled and shook his head. He shared with Parker what he knew had happened at the school. He wished he hadn't had to involve Tyler, but all he could think about was getting Natoya to safety, and while he was dealing with Cliff, he'd figured Tyler would be able to handle moving her.

"Maybe she should go stay with some friends or you until we know for sure this fucker has left town." Parker folded his arms in front of him.

Darnell appreciated his friend wanting to look out for Natoya.

"I'm heading over there now. I told her to go straight home," Darnell said.

Parker gave a nod and tapped the top of his truck. "Again, if you need us, you know we're a call away."

Darnell felt damn good about the men he worked for.

"Thanks, I appreciate it," he said. He sat forward, remembering his conversation with Dane. Since he had Parker's attention at the moment, he may as well bring his brother up. "My brother, Dane, was let go by the Fergusons. You think you have room for one more hand?"

"For your brother, I'm sure we can. Have him give me a call." Parker backed away from the truck and tipped his hat to Darnell. "Now go take care of your woman."

"You got it, boss." Darnell gave Parker a short salute.

"And stop calling me boss before I whip your ass," Parker threatened.

Darnell grinned and threw his truck in reverse. Parker turned and ambled to his home. Darnell loved to get under Parker's skin. Even though technically Parker was one of his bosses, he hated for Darnell to call him such.

Darnell navigated his way off the Blazing Eagle, and once he was on the main highway road, he headed into town. He figured it was getting late and he was sure Natoya was hungry. That woman never turned down food when he offered. He'd grab them a bite to eat, and then they were going to have to have a serious talk.

He hit the hands-free button on his steering

wheel and instructed his phone to call Natoya. It rang a couple of times before she answered.

"Hello?"

Her husky voice sent his heart racing. He didn't know what he would have done if she had been injured. The deputies had offered to have both of them checked out by the EMTs, but they'd refused. Darnell didn't need anyone to tell him to throw a bag of ice or a frozen bag of peas on his hand. Add in a couple of Tylenols for the discomfort and he'd be fine.

"Hey, I'm on my way to your house. I'll pick us up some supper. What do you have a taste for?" he asked. He glanced down at his shirt and realized he still had the half-torn one on from earlier. Thankfully, he had his duffle bag in the back. He could change it when he stopped.

"Darnell." Natoya sighed.

He didn't like the way she'd said his name at that moment. He frowned and tightened his grip on the steering wheel. There was something off in her voice.

"What's wrong, Natoya?" he asked.

"I... Don't worry about coming over here today," she said softly.

He instantly recognized her damn walls going

up. He shook his head, even though she couldn't see him.

"I'm coming, Natoya. You are not shutting me out."

"Look, there is a lot on my mind and—"

"We are going to talk about it all when I get there," he interjected. He refused to allow her to just push him off to the side. Why did this woman not understand how much he cared for her? How much he loved her?

He blinked at the notion.

He was in love with Natoya, and he was going to tell her exactly how he felt.

"Why are you so damn stubborn?" she asked.

"Why can't you let me take care of you?" he shot back. How dare she try to claim he was stubborn. She was, too. He pressed his foot down on the gas. The engine roared, and the truck picked up speed. "Now tell me what you want to eat and I'll go get it."

"Ribs. Barbecue ribs."

DARNELL ARRIVED AT NATOYA'S HOUSE AND parked his car. He got out and grabbed the food bags from the back of his cab. He'd stopped at the best barbecue spot in town and bought them dinner. He walked up to her front door and rang the bell. It didn't take long for Natoya to open it. He brushed past her and went into the house.

"Darnell." She closed the door and trailed behind him.

He went directly into the kitchen and placed the food on the island. He grimaced and stalked over to her fridge and opened the freezer. His gaze landed on a bag of frozen peas. He pulled it out and gently placed it on his knuckles before he turned to her. The coldness felt good on his swollen skin. She stood in the doorway and eyed him.

"I was able to get everything you wanted and then some," he said.

Natoya didn't say a word as she stared at him. He sensed she was about to say something he wasn't going to like.

He motioned to the food. "We can eat then talk."

"Why can't we talk now?"

"Why can't we eat and talk?" He tilted his head and met her gaze.

She tried narrowing her eyes on him, but it didn't do anything for him. It may work on her students, but not him. She called him stubborn, but she truly didn't know how far he would go to get his way.

She padded across the kitchen and stopped in front of the island where the bags were parked.

"Why do you always get so much food? Who are you trying to feed?" she grumbled. She began going through the bags and pulling stuff out. She set the containers down on the counter as she checked them.

"There's nothing wrong with leftovers. We won't have to worry about dinner tomorrow," he replied. He would probably eat everything he got for himself today. After the day he'd had, he was famished.

She opened up one of the containers that was for her. She reached in the bag and took out the plastic cutlery and napkins. She motioned to the food.

"Are you not going to eat?" She arched an eyebrow at him.

He jerked his head toward her.

"Go ahead and start. I'm right here," he said. He kept the bag on his knuckles. His hand ached, and the skin was tight. He tried to slowly close his hand into a fist but couldn't. It would take a few days to start healing. Punching that son of a bitch in the face was worth the pain.

"About earlier today, thank you," she whispered. She used the fork and stabbed it into the macaroni and cheese.

She didn't look up at him, and it bothered him.

"You don't have to thank me for defending you. That nut lost his fucking mind."

"I know. He's never been that bad before," Natoya said. She picked up the fork and placed the food in her mouth. A slight moan slipped from her. She took another bite of food and continued chewing.

"So, he's put his hands on you before? The fucker hit you?" Rage like nothing he'd ever known filled him. Had he'd known this before, the deputies would have had to pry him off Cliff.

"Not really," she said.

What the hell did that mean? Either he did or he didn't. There was no in between on the subject matter. She closed her eyes and stared at the counter. He moved over to where she was and tossed the bags of peas on the counter.

"Look, talking about my relationship with Cliff is hard for me, okay? I'm trying."

"I see that, and I appreciate it, but one thing

I want you to know is that you are not alone. I'm here, and if I have to step in again with Cliff, then I will—"

"Darnell, just stop." She flicked her gaze to him and faced him. She studied him for a moment before she began speaking again. "I told you that I didn't want you involved. I didn't want you to get hurt. I know Cliff. Something was off about him—"

"Don't make excuses for a grown man." Darnell raked his fingers through his hair with his good hand.

It irritated him that she would try to make excuses for him. That son of a bitch knew exactly what he was doing. He didn't drive all the way down to Shady Springs for nothing. He wanted Natoya back and was just going take her.

"I'm not. I'm just saying that I've known him for years and I've never seen him like this. Has he come to me and demanded that we get back together? Yes. Have I taken him back? Plenty of times. This time when I told him no, he sort of snapped."

Darnell reached up to touch her, but his hand stopped midair when she flinched. A pain went through his chest. He dropped his hand and tried not to curse out loud. This was going south fast, and he didn't like it. Brick by brick, her walls were going back up.

"Natoya." He wanted to hold her and protect her from the world.

She glanced up at him and shook her head.

"I told myself that I wouldn't date another man like Cliff. That I would stay far away from them. It's been a year since Cliff and I broke up, and I finally felt like it was time to try again. I had it all in my head what type of man I should be looking for and which ones I would be avoiding." She reached up with a shaky hand and brushed her hair from her face and tucked it behind her ear. A shaky laugh escaped her. "Then I met you."

He took a step back as if someone had slammed a two-by-four to his stomach. What the hell did that mean? He was nothing like Cliff. She had to know that by now. They'd spent so much time together in the past couple of weeks, she had to know the real him.

"Are you trying to compare me to him?" He narrowed his eyes on her. There was no way he was hearing what he thought he'd just heard her say.

"You both work on ranches. You both started out nice. Then he started fighting other men over me. He became overly possessive of me. I just can't do this—" Her voice ended on a sob. She reached up and covered her mouth with her hands. Tears fell from her eyes and slid down her soft skin.

He couldn't avoid touching her any longer. He reached for her, but she stepped back away from him. His heart pounded. How did they go from having a good time with each other to right here in this moment where she was accusing him of being exactly like the man she had run from?

What the hell was going on?

"Natoya, you know I'm nothing like him. What does us both working on a ranch have to do with anything?" He was lost on that notion. They lived in Colorado, and there were plenty of ranches and farms in their entire state. She just wasn't making any damn sense.

"How long before I see your true colors? Before you be like him—"

"I'm not like him!" he roared.

Her eyes went wide, and she took another step back away from him. He ran a hand along his face and tried to calm down. Frustration filled him that she could stand there and even think that he and Cliff were one and the same. He didn't like the fear that crept in her eyes. He looked away from her and didn't know what else he could do at this moment.

"I better go."

He stalked past her and headed for the front door. Darnell refused to glance at her. He would never beg a woman to be with him. It was obvious she had made up her mind about him. He swung open the door and shut it behind him. He jogged down the stairs and got into his truck.

Darnell was truly at a loss for words. Again, he'd trusted his heart and followed it.

Movement by the front window caught his attention. The front curtain shifted to the side. She was watching him.

Hell, she hadn't even tried to stop him from leaving. He hit the start button to turn his truck on and threw it in reverse. Once he was on the street, he took off like a bat out of hell. How did he fix this shit? What else could he have done to make Natoya see that he was who he was?

He turned off the radio and rolled down his windows to let the air flow in. Right now, he needed to think. Time would tell what would come between them.

❧ 20 ❧

Natoya let herself into her house and shut the door behind her. It had been almost a week since Darnell had stormed out. She kicked off her shoes and dropped her bag onto the couch and went into her bedroom and stripped her work clothes off. She stopped in front of the mirror and stared at her reflection.

This past week had allowed her to come to one conclusion.

She was miserable.

Darnell had burst into her life and become a part of it. She hadn't realized how much so until he was no longer calling around. Her house seemed quieter without him. Almost empty.

Hell, she felt empty.

She threw on an oversized t-shirt and shorts then went into the kitchen to see what she could eat. Nothing interested her lately. Most days she had to force herself to eat. She stood before the fridge, and nothing appealed to her. There was a small bowl of tuna fish she had made the other day. She snagged that and found some round crackers in her pantry.

She padded her way into the living room and flopped down on her couch. She grabbed the remote and flipped on the television to try to find something to watch. She scooped a little of the tuna fish out with a cracker and popped it into her mouth. For the past week the scenario in her kitchen replayed over and over in her mind. She regretted every word that had come out of her mouth. The more she thought about it, the more she knew deep down inside that Darnell was nowhere anything like Cliff.

Why had she insinuated so?

Her hand trembled as she held the bowl. She blew out a deep breath and set the bowl and crackers on the coffee table. She reached over and dug into her bag and found her cellphone. Her breaths were coming short and fast. There was one person she needed to call. Someone she knew who wouldn't judge her.

Emme.

"Hey, bestie. What's up?" Emme answered the call.

"Emme. I fucked up." Natoya sniffed. She stared at the television but didn't see a damn thing. Her brain was going a mile a minute. She had ruined a good thing with Darnell. She had let her fear of repeating history take over her. She had been so set in not getting involved with a man like Cliff that she had let it blind her to the truth.

"What's wrong?" Emme immediately grew serious.

Natoya knew she could count on her friend. She just wished she was here, but a telephone call would have to do. Emme's voice was already calming her down.

"I messed up with Darnell. I think we're done," she whispered. Her vision blurred from the unshed tears that appeared. She didn't care. The first one fell, then the next. Before she knew it, sobs racked her body. She couldn't help it. The pain of being taken advantage of over and over came to the forefront, the fear that no one would love her how she needed to be loved, the reality that she could have had that with Darnell, but she'd pushed him away.

"Calm down. Breathe, Natoya. Tell me what happened." Emme's soothing voice came through the phone.

She allowed Natoya to cry it out for a few minutes before she began speaking. Natoya used the bottom of her shirt to wipe her face. Her eyes felt swollen and gritty. She inhaled sharply and began to catch Emme up with the messages he had been sending her and the day Cliff had showed up at the school.

"Oh my God. He's lost his mind. I had heard he'd gotten arrested but I didn't even inquire on why."

"Emme, I've never seen him like that with me before." Natoya sniffed. She pushed her hair out of her face.

The sheriff's department had been in contact with her again. They were moving forward with the charges brought forth on Cliff. He had been released from jail and was warned about contacting her. Apparently, his family's reach was not going to work down here in Shady Springs.

"Okay, so Darnell stepped in, saved you, whipped Cliff's ass. Sounds like I owe Darnell a couple bottles of wine."

"I'm not done with the story yet." Natoya cringed. She continued on and got to the part of them in her kitchen. Pain spread through her chest as she got to the bit where she'd basically told Darnell he was no different than Cliff. The tears flowed again at the memory of Darnell's expression. The hurt, the anger, and disbelief on his face haunted her thoughts.

She had really hurt him.

It went without saying. She didn't know how to fix this or if she could.

"Oh no, Natoya. Why would you say things like that to him?"

"I don't know, Emme. It was like once I started talking I couldn't stop. I don't know if it was because of what had just happened with Cliff or what. But I told him not to come by. That I need time, but he wouldn't listen. He came anyway. I had just wanted a moment to myself to process what had just happened, but he didn't want me to be alone."

"As you shouldn't have been. Your ex was belligerent and was trying to kidnap you. That in itself is traumatic. Someone should have been with you. If I couldn't be, I'm glad Darnell tried to be."

Natoya rested back on the couch and stared at the ceiling. All she had wanted was to take back everything she'd said. If none of those words had been uttered, she wouldn't be sitting in her quiet house by herself crying her heart out.

"How do I fix this mess?" Natoya sighed. She rubbed her eyes and readjusted herself on the couch. She just wanted Darnell back. She needed him here with her. She wanted to feel his strong arms around her, smell his cologne, hear his voice and his laugh.

She blinked.

Was she in love with him?

Did love do this to a person? She had always thought she'd been in love in the past, but now she understood what she'd had before was not love. Now that she was apart from Darnell, her eyes were wide open.

She had fallen in love with him and hadn't even realized it.

"Well, first you need to admit that you were wrong. You need to go to him and talk it all out with him. Share with him your fears, what you need, and for God's sake, please apologize to the man," Emme said.

Her heavy sigh could be felt through the phone. Natoya remained silent as she thought about what Emme had just recommended. She could do this.

"And you know what else you need to think about doing?"

"What is that?"

"You should go see a therapist. You've been through a lot with Cliff. You need to work through all the issues you have."

"But I like talking things through with you," Natoya said.

"But I'm not a professional. I may offer good advice, but that don't mean I listen to my own words." Emme gave a dry chuckle.

Natoya smiled. Her friend was probably right. When she'd left Cliff for good, she hadn't sought any type of professional help. She'd just assumed that since she had moved and left him, she would be able to get on with her life. She had planned to dive into work and live her life.

That, apparently, had been the wrong idea.

"What would I do without you, Emme?" Natoya asked.

"Hopefully you'll never find out."

"PLEASE HAVE A SEAT, AND DR. JAMES WILL BE with you momentarily," the receptionist said.

She took the tablet from Natoya. She had a warm smile and made Natoya feel welcomed. She nervously sat in a chair in the corner of the waiting room. After she had checked in for her appointment, they'd had her complete a survey on the tablet. She'd answered all of the questions truthfully. There was no point in lying on the questionnaire. She was here to get help.

Natoya had to have a substitute cover for her this morning while she attended her first therapy appointment. She had listened to her friend. Emme was highly intelligent and was always a great ear to lean on, but she was right. It was time for Natoya to get professional help. She'd searched high and low and was pleasantly surprised to find that Shady Springs had several mental health practices in town.

She stared down at her phone and contemplated calling Darnell. But what would she say?

I'm fucked up in the head. Please take me back.

She bit back a snort at the thought. If only it would be that easy. She had hurt Darnell. The man just wanted to be with her. He wanted her, and she'd pushed him away. She hadn't wanted to allow him to claim her as his woman. It was glaringly obvious that he wanted her. That he wanted to be able to call Natoya his girlfriend. But he honored her wishes. She sniffed and closed her eyes.

If she went to him, would he take her back? If the shoe was on the other foot, would *she* take *him* back? A sharp pain pierced Natoya's heart. If she had lost Darnell for good, she would have to get over him. She could. It would take her a long time to piece herself together, but it was doable. She blinked back the tears that threatened to fall. She was going to get through this. She was taking the right step.

"Miss Grant?" An older woman with a short blonde pixie cut and red-framed glasses stood in the doorway.

"Yes, that's me." Natoya stood from her chair and strode across the room. She followed the woman through a winding hallway.

"I'm Dr. James. I do apologize, my assistant who normally assists me is out sick." She smiled and stopped in front of an office door. She opened it and waved Natoya inside. She entered the office that had a small couch seated near a desk with a desktop computer. It had simple decor and a window with a perfect view that overlooked the pond in the front of the building.

Natoya took a seat on the couch and waited for Dr. James. The therapist sat at the desk and typed out a few commands on her computer before she turned to Natoya with a welcoming smile.

"We are just going to start with a series of questions. Relax and breathe. We won't even touch on any of the hard stuff today," Dr. James announced.

Natoya gave a nod and felt a little relief. She wasn't sure what to expect out of these appointments. She just prayed that this woman could help her.

"Have you ever been to a therapist before or been under the care of a psychiatrist?"

"No, I haven't. This is my first time," Natoya admitted.

"Good for you for making the first step in improving your mental health. Let me explain what we can offer here for you." Dr. James went on to describe the practice, how they were able to meet the needs of the town, and the flexibility they offered.

Everything sounded good to Natoya. With it being her first time, she didn't know what to expect.

"How does that all feel?"

"Wonderful. This practice has thought about everything a person would need," Natoya said.

She had read about some of what the doctor had spoken about on their website. She had been impressed with all they were able to treat and cover.

"Now I must ask you the hardest question that you will get today." Dr. James offered a smile. She leaned back in her chair and eyed Natoya. "What is it you wish to accomplish in coming here?"

Natoya typed out a few commands on her classroom desktop. She stared at the screen for a moment before she continued with what she was working on. The class was currently taking a quiz. She gazed around the room at the students. She had regretted not taking the entire day off. She had plenty of vacation days she could have pulled from. After leaving the therapy appointment, she'd had a lot on her mind.

Mainly Darnell.

Her gaze landed on Tyler who pushed up from his desk and walked to hers.

"Hey, Tyler," she said. She tilted her head to the side and noticed that he appeared a little off.

"Hi, Miss Grant," he mumbled. He set his paper down in the basket on her desk.

Something was wrong.

"Is there something wrong?" she asked softly. She didn't want to speak too loudly. If she needed to take him outside in the hall for a little privacy, she would.

He sniffed and turned his gray eyes onto her.

"There was an accident on the ranch yesterday," Tyler said.

Natoya's heart leaped. She knew that ranch life was no easy life and things happened all the time. She glanced around the classroom and found the other students were still working on their quiz.

"Is everyone okay?" she asked Tyler. Her heart pounded as she waited for his answer. She bit her lip.

"Yeah. Darnell was out riding Benji, and somehow when they were out, Benji messed up his leg. The doctor was supposed to come today to see him," Tyler said.

The bottom of Natoya's stomach gave way. She immediately felt the direct urge to get up and leave. Darnell loved that horse so much. She had to go to him. She didn't know if he would want her there or not, but she had to check in on Benji and Darnell. She couldn't even begin to imagine what he was going through. That was his faithful horse who had been with him for years.

The rest of the day crept by. Even with her taking half a day to go to her therapy appointment, the afternoon seemed to drag by. Once the kids were let out, Natoya wasn't going to finish anything else. She was going to drive out to the Blazing Eagle. She was sure that's where Darnell would be.

She packed up her belongings and practically raced out of the classroom. Once in her car, she headed straight to the ranch. Lucky enough, today she had dressed casual in jeans, a nice blouse, and a cardigan sweater.

She squeezed the steering wheel as she drove out to the ranch. Her nerves got the best of her. She just prayed that Darnell didn't lose his horse. That would tear him apart. She thought about how silly the two were together. That horse cared for Darnell as well. It was evident by the way Benji treated him. She thought back to the day when Darnell had kissed her and Benji jumped in thinking he was harming her. She laughed at Benji's actions. He had been smart enough to grab Darnell's hair and pull him away from her.

When she arrived at the Blazing Eagle, she

followed the road signs to the barn. She couldn't think of anything else but getting to Darnell. Once she arrived at the big structure, she parked her vehicle and blew out a deep breath. If she walked in there and Darnell sent her away, then she would leave. She probably didn't deserve to be there with him during this time, but she needed to talk with him.

She needed to come clean with him and share the feelings she was harboring for him.

"Here goes nothing," she murmured. She opened the door and stepped out of the car. She headed toward the barn. If he was not there, she'd go find someone and ask them where he was. She wasn't going to leave until she'd at least spoken with Darnell.

"HEY, DR. HUTSON. THANKS FOR COMING out," Darnell greeted the vet with a firm handshake.

They walked into the barn and stopped by Benji's stall.

"It's my pleasure. I'm sorry I couldn't get out here last night. I had so many emergency farm calls. At least four were due to breeched cows in labor, and then there was a horse with a deep shoulder wound that I needed to stitch up. Damn thing bled like crazy, and then we couldn't figure out how the damn animal got it."

"Wow." Darnell opened Benji's stall to allow the doctor to go inside.

Benji stood up, but he held his front right leg up in the air. He wouldn't put weight on it. Darnell combed his fingers through his hair as the doctor spoke low to Benji. His horse should be familiar with Dr. Hutson. Darnell eyed the horse to ensure he wouldn't do anything crazy like attack the good doctor.

Guilt ate at Darnell. This was all his fault. He'd taken Benji out and ridden him hard. His horse loved when he could just run free.

It had been two weeks since he'd seen or spoken with Natoya. He just couldn't fathom that she thought he was like Cliff. He figured they'd both just needed to take a breather from each other. But he had to admit his pride had taken a hit and he was hurt. Her accusation had cut him deep.

To blow off steam, he'd saddled Benji, and they'd gone out far on the ranch. Once they'd got to this one part where there was open flat land,

Darnell had allowed Benji to just go. There had been an unseen hole in the ground that Benji stepped in, and it sent him and Darnell flying through the air. Darnell had been lucky and hit the ground in one spot and Benji landed opposite him. Had Benji landed on him, he'd probably be in the hospital.

Darnell focused on the vet as he assessed Benji. He just hoped and prayed his horse would be okay. Darnell, on the other hand, was sore. He'd hit the ground hard. He wasn't as young as he used to be. There was a time he could be thrown from a horse and walk away with no aches and pains.

Now? His muscles were stiff, and he ached everywhere.

"Well, good news, I don't think it's broken," Dr. Hutson said. He glanced up from where he was bent down near Benji. He ran his hand along his leg and shook his head. "Not broken. I'd say a pretty tough sprain but not broken. We need to wrap it up. Once it's stable, he'll be able to put weight on it. No running for at least six weeks to allow it to heal. Daily wrappings, and it should heal fine."

Darnell blew out a deep breath and ran a hand along his face. He had been so worried about Benji.

He'd thought he was going to lose him. Dr. Hutson came out of the stall and rifled through his bag he had left outside the stall. He found some wrapping tape and motioned for Darnell to join him.

Between the two of them, Benji allowed his leg to be wrapped. He didn't like it at first, but then he placed his leg down. He limped slightly.

"It will take him a few days to get used to it, but he will. I'll come back to check on him next week, but I'm certain that this is just a sprain."

"Thanks so much, Doc." Darnell held his hand out to Dr. Hutson. He was grateful that there was nothing else wrong with his horse. A sprain they could handle.

"If you need anything else, just give me a call." The vet grabbed his bag from outside the stall and disappeared out of sight.

Darnell rubbed Benji's neck. He blew out a deep breath. He'd forgotten to grab a couple of carrots for Benji. He turned around and froze in place. He blinked and focused on the figure standing in the doorway of Benji's stall.

"Natoya. What are you doing here?" he asked. He greedily took her in. She looked damn good in her jeans and blouse. Her brown skin practically glowed, and her warm eyes held a hesitation in them. Just seeing her in the flesh revealed how much he'd truly missed her.

"I heard Benji was injured, and I wanted to check in on him and you," she said. She held up two carrots she must have gotten out of the treat bag he kept hanging near the entrance to the barn. Her gaze dropped to Benji's leg. "He's not going to lose his leg, is he? Or have to be put down?"

"No. According to the doctor, it's just a sprain," he shared. He had yet to take his eyes off her. He was touched that she had thought so much of his horse that she'd wanted to come check in on him.

"Can I give these to him?"

He jerked his head in a nod. She stepped forward and moved to where Benji was standing. His horse had picked up on her as well and released a neigh. He blew out a deep breath before biting off the first carrot. Another couple of bites, and the large carrot was gone.

"You sure do love you some carrots, don't you?" Natoya murmured. She held out the other one for him.

Benji promptly ate that. She laughed and patted him on his neck. She turned to face

Darnell. She folded her hands in front of her and glanced down at the floor.

"You're only here to check in on Benji?" he asked.

She shook her head. She came to stand in front of him. It took everything he had to not reach for her. He should be mad at her, he shouldn't want her like he did. One look at her, and all the feelings he had for her came rushing back.

"I did come to check in on Benji, but you as well. I know how much he means to you," she said. She took his hand in hers and closed the gap between them.

He should have stepped back away from her, but his feet were not cooperating at the moment.

"I wanted to be here with you if something tragic had happened to Benji."

"Why?" he asked.

She tilted her head back to meet his gaze. "Because I'm in love with you, Darnell Murphy."

The air in his lungs escaped as if someone had suctioned it all out. He paused and stared down at her. He couldn't have heard what he thought he'd heard. Did she just say she loved him?

"I know the last time we saw each other, I said some hurtful things. I'm here to ask you for your forgiveness. I was experiencing a storm of emotions and I wasn't thinking straight. I should have never compared you to Cliff. I don't know how I can right this wrong, but I want to say that I'm sorry." She lifted his hand and used the back of it to rub along her cheek.

Unable to resist touching her any longer, he cupped the back of her neck. He breathed in her floral scent from her perfume.

"All I ever wanted from the moment we met was to make you smile, make you happy, and make you mine," Darnell said. He rested his forehead on hers. There was so much he wanted to say to her, but here in a horse's stall was not the place. "These two weeks without you have been torturous. I can't live without you, Natoya. I need you in my life."

"And I need you," Natoya whispered. She opened her eyes, and big fat teardrops teetered on her eyelids. She blinked, and the twin tears flowed down her cheeks.

"I waited so long to be able to hear you say that you love me. Natoya Grant, I am in love with you and have been for a while," he admitted.

"You love me?" Natoya gasped.

"Did you really have any doubts?" he asked.

"After what I said, yeah. I figured I had ruined

any chance I had with you. I half expected you to yell for me to get out of here," she said. Natoya gripped his shirt and turned her brown eyes on him. "Emme talked me into going to therapy. She thought it may help me deal with the issues I have. My first appointment was today."

"That is great, pretty lady." He cupped her face in his hands and lowered his lips to hers.

The kiss began soft and tantalizing. Natoya's lips were as satiny as he remembered. She sighed into the kiss, allowing his tongue to sweep inside.

He wanted this woman before him. She had been brave to come to him and apologize. He could put it all aside now that she was here. He understood she had a lot to deal with, but she was going to learn that he was here for her. He cared about her and her wellbeing. Their kiss grew deeper. He tilted his head to the side so he could continue to taste and tease her.

Natoya groaned and gasped. He broke the kiss and stared down into her lust-filled eyes.

"We need open communication between us at all time," he murmured.

She jerked her head in a nod of agreement. He brushed her bottom lip with his thumb. Her mouth was slightly swollen from his kiss.

"Natoya, I'm just a man who is in love with

you. This man will never lie to you and will always be there to protect you. Can you deal with that?"

"Yes. These past two weeks have been torture. I hadn't realized how much I needed you until you were gone," she whispered.

"Well, if you are willing to have me, I won't be going anywhere," he said.

"Please don't leave me again," she said.

"I hadn't left you. I only gave us space, but believe me, pretty lady, you're going to be stuck with me. I'm not going anywhere." He pressed another kiss to her lips and lifted his head. "Now tell me you love me again."

"Darnell Murphy. I love you."

EPILOGUE

"Look at this sun. It's on its way down," Natoya exclaimed.

The big orange ball was slowly descending toward the horizon. Natoya grew excited watching the sun descend. It had been a long time since she had taken the time to watch it. Darnell dismounted from Benji and came to her where she sat on top of Mavis. She and Mavis had bonded so much that they had borrowed her so Natoya could go riding.

"Recognize the area?" Darnell said. He helped her dismount Mavis.

Her body slid along his on the way to the ground. He kept his hands on her waist as she looked around.

"Is this the same spot where we made love for

the first time?" Natoya asked. It had been six months since that day. She smiled and took in the beautiful rolling acres. She absolutely loved coming out here and taking in the picturesque scenery.

Since Benji had injured his leg he had made a full recovery. Natoya and Darnell had made great strides in their relationship. She had officially declared herself Darnell's girlfriend. Anywhere they went, she introduced herself as Darnell's girlfriend. She couldn't help it. She was so in love with this man that she didn't want to take him for granted. She tried to ensure that he knew how much she loved him.

Cliff had been hit with so many charges that he'd ended up taking a plea deal. She hadn't had to worry about him ever since he'd been arrested. No more text messages and no more surprise visits from him.

"Come. Let's go have a seat. It should set completely in about ten minutes."

"Are you sure we shouldn't be going now before it gets dark?" Natoya asked.

She followed him and took a seat on the grassy knoll. The two horses ignored them and went about their business and grazed. Darnell had been taking her out to ride at least once a week. She enjoyed their time out on horseback. It was one of her favorite pastimes. Darnell sat next to her and grinned.

"We'll be fine. It's a straight shot back to the barn. I know my way around. You'll be safe with me." He had the nerve to toss her a wink.

Natoya glanced at the sky and took in the beautiful colors that were painted across it, as if it were a canvas. She leaned her head on his shoulder and watched the sun continue to descend. It was breathtakingly beautiful.

"That's just so amazing." She sighed.

Their day had been so fun and peaceful. After the trek back to the barn, they would return the horses, then head out. She had planned to spend the night at Darnell's house. They rotated between each other's residences. She wasn't sure why, but at the moment it worked for them. Eventually, she was sure they would start talking about moving in with each other.

The sun had officially set, but the sky was still light out. She watched as Darnell turned to her and knelt in front of her.

"What are you doing?" She giggled.

He pulled a small black box from his pocket, and she froze in place, unable to take her eyes off the object in his hand.

Her smile disappeared. "Is that what I think it is?"

He cleared his throat and opened the box. Nestled inside was a princess-cut diamond solitaire ring. Natoya's eyes blurred from the tears that came forward. She sniffed and rubbed her eyes.

"Natoya Grant, these past few months have been everything I could ever have imagined. You've taught me patience and what true love is. I'm so happy that you are in my life. I love you so much and I need you with me forever. Will you marry me?"

Natoya shifted to kneel in front of Darnell. Her tears flowed down her face, and she stared into the face of the man she loved more than life itself. This man had more patience than any person she had ever met. Her cowboy had lassoed her heart, and she didn't want to get away from him.

Ever.

Her smile grew wide. She thought of the little secret she had been carrying. He wasn't the only one who had something to present.

"Yes, Darnell. Yes, I'll marry you."

He released a whoop and scooped her up. He swung them around, and she scream and held on tight.

"Don't drop me." She giggled.

He put her down, and she held out her hand for him to slip the ring on her finger. It was a perfect fit. She wondered how he had known her ring size. She couldn't stop looking at it.

Darnell tipped her chin upward and covered her mouth with his for a hard kiss. She wrapped her arms around his neck. The kiss was possessive and demanding. Natoya turned herself over to the kiss and returned it with the same fervor he gave her. Remembering what she had to share with him, she pulled back slightly. Darnell's arms were still around her, keeping her against him.

"What is it?" he asked. He softly kissed her lips. He peppered small kisses along her cheeks and along her neck.

"There's something I need to share with you." She laughed.

He lifted his head and gazed at her. He raised an eyebrow at her. She took his hand and rested it on her belly.

"You've offered to give me your last name, well, you've given us something else as well."

He paused for a minute with a confused look. Then his gaze dropped to her stomach where she'd placed his hand. His eyes went wide.

"Are you saying that you're...um.."

It was one of the first times she had seen Darnell speechless.

"Darnell, we're pregnant," she whispered.

He cupped her face with his hands and studied her. He sniffed, then kissed her forehead, then her nose, and finally, her lips.

"I love you, Natoya Grant." He took her lips again in a searing hot kiss that was short-lived. He took her by the hand and started dragging her to the horses. "Come. Let's go back to my place so we can celebrate properly."

A NOTE FROM THE AUTHOR

Dear reader,

Thank you for reading Lasso My Heart. I have been dying to get back to the Blazing Eagle Ranch. Now that I've returned to Shady Springs, I sort of don't want to leave. Darnell was supposed to be the last book but I'm thinking there are more cowboys who need some good loving!

Want more from the Blazing Eagle? Leave a review and let me know it!

Happy reading,

Peyton Banks

P.S. On a cowboy high right now and looking for more? Then head over to my shared world, The

Silver Creek Ranch (www.silvercreekcowboys.com) and start that series today!

WRANGLING HER COWBOY
SILVER CREEK RANCH 1

A broken cowboy...his shining light. Will she be enough to pull him out of the darkness?

Draven Harvey came home to Ironhaven, South Dakota, to settle down. The retired Marine was done with serving his country and just wanted a peaceful life working his father's ranch. The Silver Creek Ranch was for men like him—broken and needing help finding their place in society.

After his time in the military, he wants to be left alone. Ranching was to be his life.

Cashea Moss took notice of the grumpy town hero who came to the bar where she sang every weekend. She was new to town, but she'd heard plenty about Draven. His eyes were intense and held tales of horror she was sure he had experienced during deployments. There was something about him that made her want to see him smile.

Draven tried to fight the attraction he felt for Cashea, but she quickly dismantled the barriers he had constructed around himself. He couldn't get her out of his mind after one steamy night. Her soft touch made him want to do things he'd sworn he wouldn't do—become a protector and fall in love.

Wrangling Her Cowboy is a steamy interracial BWWM romance with a broken small town hero, a beautiful heroine and a HEA.

Want to start the Silver Creek Ranch series? Go to www.silvercreekcowboys.com and start this multi-author shared world!

ABOUT THE AUTHOR

USA TODAY bestselling author, Peyton Banks, is the alter ego of a city girl who is a romantic at heart. Her mornings consist of coffee and daydreaming up the next steamy romance book ideas. She loves spinning romantic tales of hot alpha males and the women they love. Make sure you check her out!

Sign up for Peyton's Newsletter to find out the latest releases, giveaways and news!

Want to know the latest about Peyton Banks? Follow her online:

tiktok.com/@peytonbanks_author

facebook.com/peytonbanksauthor

goodreads.com/peytonbanks

bookbub.com/profile/peyton-banks

instagram.com/peytonbanks_author

bsky.app/profile/authorpeytonbanks.bsky.social

amazon.com/author/peytonbanks

ALSO BY PEYTON BANKS

Dallas

Dalton